Koa of the Drowned Kingdom

by Ryan Campbell

Koa of the Drowned Kingdom

Production copyright FurPlanet Productions © 2015

Cover Artwork © Cooner 2015
http://cooner.johntoons.com

Published by FurPlanet Productions
Dallas, Texas
www.FurPlanet.com

ISBN 978-1-61450-270-8

Printed in the United States of America
First Edition Trade Paperback 2015

Table of Contents

Thanks to my readers, Kevin Frane, Watts Martin, and Tim Susman.

Thanks to John Nunnemacher for his wonderful art.

Thanks to Puckles for being a feisty little jerk of a rabbit.

And thanks to my husband David, who is the kindest soul I've ever met.

Chapter 1

Koa swayed upside down over the waters of Titan, searching for any ripples of brown beneath the low waves. Tug had been down there a long time. He tried to track the rising bubbles of air, but the gentle ebb and wash of the incoming tide scattered them. He wasn't too worried; Tug knew his way around the murky waters of the Toes. All the same, he gave the rope hooked in his wing-fingers a gentle pull to find any slack. There wasn't any.

The rope ladder to which he clung shook, and he gripped it more tightly with his toes. Above him, thousands of feet tall, the mighty mangrove swayed in the ocean breeze. This was Titan, and of all the Kingdoms, it was easily the largest and mightiest. But because of its massive size, the tree caught more of the wind, and was always in motion, bowing and dancing before the endless expanse of the Southern Sea. Looking up, Koa could see its powerful arms stretching out over the water, heavy with green leaves and ripening fruit, lights twinkling in the settlements on the eastern boughs where night's shadow already fell. Still higher, he could make out the Crown of Titan, where all the flying foxes lived. All but him.

"Hey! Breeze-for-brains! You're supposed to be paying attention." He looked down to see Tug's grinning head poking up from the water, droplets streaming from his bushy whiskers.

"Sorry," he said. "I was just—"

"I know what you were just. Head in the game, tree rat! If I get et, this is gonna be a lot harder for you!"

"Any sign of it yet?" Koa asked, trying to keep the hope from his voice.

Tug shook his head. "Plenty o' oysters."

"But no necklace."

"It's a fiddly little bit of silver what dropped down into a giant ocean, you know. Like lookin' for a needle in a mudstack. You want to come down and have a scrounge?"

"I would," Koa said, rubbing his chin. "But you're just so much better at grubbing around in the mud than I am."

"It's a lot of mudding work for some stuffy bat what ain't even your boyfriend yet," Tug grumbled.

"And what are you all of a sudden? Employed?"

The otter grinned, spat a thin ribbon of water that came nowhere close to hitting Koa, and dove below the surface again.

His rippling figure kicked and twisted beneath the water and the Toes of Titan, great roots that jutted up from the swamp like stalagmites, and then a wave came in and washed him from view.

The time passed, and Koa tried to keep focused on the water as Tug's movements below drew his safety rope back and forth. Koa always wondered how it was that Tug never tangled his safety rope around the Toes or any of the other detritus below, but he always came up with the line free and clear, ready to be reeled in like a fish and hoisted back up to the ladder.

Bats were built to hang upside down, their toes long, clawed, and powerful. Virtually nothing could shake his grip free. So it was his job to cling to the ladder, be ready to haul the otter back in, and to keep a careful watch for—

He frowned. A little distance away, the V of a ripple moved across the water at an angle to the waves. He peered more closely.

There was a shadow. It might be a piece of driftwood. A knobbly bit poked out of the water, but then it sank beneath, the shadow vanishing.

Crocodile.

This was very bad news. Otters were fast, but crocs were faster, and if the size of that shadow was any indication, this one was enormous. Koa squeezed his toes, clenching the rope tightly, and hauled at the safety line, trying to find the end of the slack. It didn't take him long to find it, which was bad news, because it meant Tug was a good ways out. He gave the rope a series of sharp pulls, three in a row—their signal. He waited for Tug to yank the rope back in reply, but the line stayed steady.

Scanning the waves, he searched for the figure of the crocodile below, but couldn't see it anywhere. Maybe it had left. But of course it hadn't; it would have smelled Tug in the water. The thing had looked big, what he'd seen of it. He gave the line a good hard pull now, frightened, but this time it sagged loose in his claws. Panicking, he reeled it in faster, the coarse, wet rope rasping against his wings and fingers as he hauled.

The end of the rope came up, frayed and dripping.

"No," he breathed. "Tug?" He swung above the water, listening. He pricked his keen ears, flicking from side to side. They picked up the sounds of life in Titan above—shopping and chatter and construction—and the wind rustling through the leaves, but nearby there was only the creak of the rope ladder, the rush of the waves, and the mosquitos. Then, from beneath the water, a muffled shout.

With a loud splash, Tug broke the surface some thirty feet away, his lean, muscled body arcing through the air, spraying out fans of water. "Koa! The line!" Behind him, a massive black crocodile erupted, curling back on itself with a croaking roar, jaws gaping wide enough to swallow Tug in one bite. Water birds scattered all directions with panicked squawks.

His paws shaking, Koa pulled up the end of the rope and sent the coil sailing across the water. It unspooled as it flew, but knotted halfway down and dropped. He swore a curse under his breath; they'd practiced this so many times since the last croc, but now he couldn't do it properly to save his life. Or Tug's.

Tug furrowed his way through the water, his webbed paws paddling furiously, but the crocodile was faster and more powerful.

"He's gaining on you," Koa shouted. "Bank to the right; he's too big to turn quickly!"

With a forceful kick, the otter twisted to the side and slipped beneath the turbid water. Huge jaws carved through it just behind. The glistening black back of the crocodile insinuated a wide circle, and then, with a slap of the tail, disappeared again.

Koa muttered curses to himself as he fumbled with the wet rope, hauling it in again. If his wings were any good, he could have flown the line out to the otter, maybe even hauled him up. Some bats were strong enough to carry others. He was sure if he were able to fly, he'd do it all the time. He'd have powerful limbs and taut membranes, not these tattered and scarred strips of flesh that dangled from broken fingers.

A splash came from his right—Tug had surfaced among the thick lattice of rootlets, some finger-thin, others as big around as Tug himself, that bristled around Titan's trunk. He squirmed and nestled himself between them. With a croaking growl, the crocodile breached the water and snaked after him. Tug wriggled farther back as powerful jaws snapped and crunched, tearing away at the rootlets to get at him.

Koa looked down at the coil of rope sinking into the ocean. Of course now it would untangle itself, now that it was useless. Even if he could throw it out to Tug again, there would be no way the otter could climb up past the crocodile.

"Koa!" Tug called up to him from within the wooden cage of roots. "You're gonna have to go fishing!"

Koa stared at the monstrous croc, its reptilian tail thrashing with tremendous force as it struggled to get at the otter. "Are you kidding me?"

"Yes! I thought, hey, I'm about to be swallowed whole by a mudding sea monster. This is the perfect time for a hilarious joke!"

The croc roared and yanked its jaws backward, tearing a huge cluster of brittle roots away

Koa bit his lip. Hang it all. This, like everything else, would be so much easier with wings. Not to mention less likely to get him killed. "Okay, I'll be right back. Try to keep away from it!"

"You mean these giant slashing daggers of death here?" Tug clung to a root and clambered up out of the water, toward Titan's trunk. Below him, the toe-roots jutted upward like needles. "I think maybe I can keep that in mind!"

Muttering one last curse, Koa dropped the remaining rope, letting the line dangle down into the water again, its other end secured to the rope ladder. This he climbed as quickly as he could, using both fingers and toes.

The top of the ladder draped around the girth of one of Titan's lowest limbs, Mist Foot, a broad and powerful branch that nonetheless had few homes or buildings on it. Though it was wide and extended a very long way over the water, it was likely to catch high waves in a storm. and the mosquitos and midges were far thicker here than higher up. Not to mention, the surface of the branch was slick with algae and the detritus that fell from Titan's upper levels. Only the poorest inhabited the lower branches, and they were mostly away now, begging or working in the markets, so there was no one to bother Koa as he scurried down Mist Foot's reach.

There was extra rope here though, plenty of it, most of it used for fishing. Koa knew where all the spare rope was stored on Titan, and even in some of the other Kingdoms. Here there were several coils tucked away behind an old tackle hut. At a glance, he identified length, flexibility, and sturdiness, and he grabbed two coils, giving each a quick tug test for rot and slime mold that could make them too slippery to use. With a few deft movements of his feet—he'd always been better at tying knots with his toes than with his fingers—he knotted them together and hurried back down the branch.

The crocodile had lifted itself halfway out of the water and was pulling itself across the roots toward Tug, who had flattened himself against the trunk of the tree. The beast had looked huge enough in the water, but now, halfway out, it proved absolutely enormous. Koa almost wondered why it bothered with Tug; surely the otter would be little more than a snack.

He moved past the rope ladder, farther down the limb, until he reached a lower branch, not wide enough to walk on, much less support any buildings, and he crawled out on this a short distance, looking down until he judged himself sufficiently out over open water, and a good fifty feet away from the dangling ladder and safety line. The water looked dark and deep.

"If you've finished farting around," Tug shouted, "you might take it into consideration that your definitely favorite brother is about to be turned into crocodile poo."

Koa knotted the rope around the branch and took several deep, rapid breaths. He gripped the end of the rope tightly in his toes. Never mind that bats couldn't swim. He took a deep breath and dropped off the branch, spreading his arms.

The water slapped against his wings with a smack. That's going to sting like hell in a second, he thought, and then it did. But he was already underwater. He contorted and twisted, fighting his body's panic at being submerged. He had done this before. Granted, not with an actual crocodile in the water. He hoped, for Tug's sake, that the smack of his wings had been loud enough to attract the monster's attention, and for his sake that it hadn't. Waiting to find out, however, would be suicide. He gripped the rope in his toes and flailed to the surface, quickly sliding one foot over the other until he found the tension in the line and hauled himself out of the water.

The fang-lined gullet of a lunging crocodile met his face.

In panic, he nearly let go of the rope, some deep-buried instinct making him flap his wings in frantic desperation. The efforts were useless, of course; the air merely caught and fluttered his torn flaps of skin. He could no more fly than he could swim.

The croc veered in a wide circle, turning back toward him. The only way to safety was up. Koa climbed higher, one foot over the other. As the croc turned back toward him, he cast a quick glance toward Tug, but didn't see him amid the tangle of smashed roots, nor was he already on the safety line hanging from the ladder. He had to be in the water. If the croc lost interest in Koa now, Tug would be reptile food.

Koa gritted his teeth and paused in his ascent, grabbing the rope below him and thrashing it in the water. "Come on, you big scaly bastard," he shouted at it. "I'm over here!"

He needn't have bothered—the huge beast rose beneath him, popping up like a deadly jack-in-the-box, sprays of clear water fanning out to either side. Its mouth was yellow, its broad tongue speckled with dark spots. Koa was just above it, and could see right down its throat. He heard himself scream, a high-pitched, ear-ringing sound, and yanked himself higher on the rope, his arms spreading wide, body curling upward. The crocodile's jaws snapped closed below him, puffing the rotten-fish reek of its breath in his face, and then the creature went crashing back into the water with a tremendous splash.

Still no Tug. He hoisted himself higher on the rope, watching the crocodile turn a predatory circle beneath him. It eyed him from below, snorting fans of water from its nostrils.

He tried to calm the beating of his heart and stuck his tongue out at it. "What's the matter, ya' big dummy? Can't figure out how to get the treat on the rope?" He flicked the line hanging below him at its face, a good length of sopping rope slapping it across the skull. It roared at him, slapping its tail.

A little gasp of breath came from a short distance away, and in the corner of his vision, he saw a brown shape hoist itself out of the water, clinging to the safety line that hung from the rope ladder. Good. Just a little longer.

"That's right, dummy. Nothing you can do. You're stuck down there. Helpless." He flicked the rope again, smacking the side of the croc's face.

It opened its jaws and snapped them closed on the rope.

"Oh," he said. "Mud."

He started climbing as fast as he could, but the croc swam away with the end of the rope clamped between its jaws, pulling it out at an angle, as taut as a suspension cable. Koa hung still beneath it, the fibers of the tight rope pinching at his fingers

and toes. With jerks of its heavy head, the croc yanked the rope, bouncing Koa up and down. It was trying to shake him off.

He climbed a few inches higher. The croc gave another tug, and the rope buzzed like the twang of a lute string. His fingers slipped free, leaving him swinging out over the water, hanging on by his toes. A low creak came from the rope, its wet fibers rasping against each other. He wasn't concerned about his knot slipping—his knots always held—but how much could the rope itself hold? Five, maybe six hundred pounds. Less if it were as old as it looked. And the thrashing reptile below probably had a ton or two of powerful muscle driving it forward.

The rope was going to break. He curled up to grab at it again, right-side up this time so he could more easily see where he was going. He was barely able to hold on as the croc lashed the line back and forth, but he climbed, wing over wing, foot over foot, clinging between each ascent to avoid being thrown from the line. Then the crocodile gave another tug, fiercer than before, pulling the rope so taut it barely even shook. The sounds of rope fibers snapping came from above him. He looked up. It was the knot.

Every knot weakened a rope. An untied rope was strong, but once you bound it to something else—a boat, another rope, any-thing—you distressed the fibers, twisted them, crushed them. When a rope broke, it would break where it had been tied to another. If he could just climb above the midway knot, he would be safe. He scrambled higher and higher. The strands of the rope snapped, one by one, just below the knot. The croc gave a few fierce shakes, seeming to sense that it almost had its prey, and Koa clung tight for fear of being flung free. If only he could fly.

The crocodile reared high in the water and lunged forward, and that was enough. The rope snapped just above Koa. He gave one desperate reach for the rope above… and caught something thick and furry and wet. The end of the broken rope went looping down to the swamp floor, leaving him swinging free.

He looked up to see Tug's hindquarters just above him. His fingers were latched around the otter's ankle.

"Hullo," Tug said affably. "Mind loosening the claws there just a touch? I'm only lending you the paw, not *giving* it to you."

Chapter 2

W hew!" Tug unslung the sopping wet bag from over his shoulder and set it down heavily on the hideout floor. "Heavy! Not a bad haul this time."

"Except we didn't actually find what we were looking for. And we both nearly got eaten," Koa pointed out. He followed the otter into the wooden hollow in the knees of Titan and flopped down on the lower bunk against the far wall. The old mattress burped a musty cloud.

"Nearly. An important word, that. Difference between comedy and tragedy." Tug turned the bag on end and dumped the contents out on the floor of the hideout. They came sloughing out in a heap of swamp water and sand. "That was real brave, plopping yourself in the water like that. Didn't expect that."

"You told me to, remember?"

"Yeah, but I was—" Tug looked thoughtful. "What's the word you use? Ironic. I was bein' ironic."

Koa groaned and slumped halfway off the mattress, staring up at the ceiling. "That's not what that means."

"Oh really?" Tug pawed through the muck, plucking out fat shells and shiny bits of metal. "Then what was I, professor?"

"Scared you were gonna lose the rest of your tail."

The otter curled his stumpy tail around to eye it. It was shorter than a full-grown otter's by about a foot, the tip hairless, a gnarled mass of white scar tissue. He'd lost it a few years back, when he'd been running with a group of otters he called the LTSL—The Less Than Savory Lot. They were if not ne'er-do-wells, at least *seldom*-do-wells. Koa and his family hadn't seen Tug for nearly a year, and when he'd finally come back, he'd returned with some peculiar mannerisms, an even more peculiar accent, and an abbreviated tail. He would never say much about them, except to cheerfully mention that they'd gotten up to the very best sorts of no good, and that he'd had his fill of it. Koa had missed him desperately when he'd been gone, but on his return, Tug had acted like nothing had changed at all, and even the loss of his tail hadn't seemed to bother him.

"Naw," Tug said. "Not with my brother hanging out up there, ready to dunk his own narrow arse in the brink to save my own, eh?"

"Never again," Koa vowed. "That was too much. Next time I'm gonna let the croc eat you and wait for you to swim out the other end."

Tug stuck out his tongue. "Oi. No need to be foul. You wanna see what we got or what?"

"Yeah, okay." Koa slid the rest of the way off the mattress and crawled over to the pile of muck in the middle of the hideout. It wasn't really a hideout, of course—just a small, natural hollow in the Toes of Titan—but they'd called it their hideout ever since they'd found it as pups playing at pirates. They'd constructed rude bunks and strung a hammock along one wall, pillaging bits of discarded furniture—a nightstand, an old glowlamp—wherever they could find them. On all the walls, their treasures were hung—mostly junk that had fallen into the ocean from the world above, only to be rescued later by Tug's clever paws.

"Oysters, of course. Seven of 'em. We'll save those for last." Tug stacked the large, knobbly shells to one side. He drew a long, copper chain out of the muck. It had a round pendant at the end. "Pocket watch."

"Let me see!" Koa snatched it from his fingers and popped it open. Water and sand dribbled out onto the floor. The glass cover was clear enough that the face was still clear, and the brass still shiny, with little tarnishing. He shook it, and water sloshed around inside. "Do you think it'd work?"

Tug shrugged. "You know seawater kills the magic. You could get it re-spelled, but it's not like it costs much less than buying a new one. Here, look, this is better." He shook sand off of a small ring with green stones set in it. "Not tarnished at all. That'll be gold. And emeralds. Ruduuk will give us more than a few pennies for that, eh?"

"Sure," Koa agreed glumly, shaking the watch again.

"Oh come on, what do you want with an old watch anyway? You need to know the time all of a sudden?"

Koa sighed. "It's not that. I just—" He stared out the entrance of the hollow, up past the branches. "It looked familiar for a second. I think my father used to have a watch just like that. It'd be nice to have one too, you know? Sometimes I can almost remember what it was like to live up there."

Tug leered at him. "Yeah, I know the something up there you want."

Koa perked his ears. "Is it time already? Did we miss it?"

"Nah, don't swim outta your skin, we got time. At least time enough to open the oysters, eh?"

"Yeah, okay." He took the little knife and the gritty, black oyster Tug proffered.

Tug held the oyster in his lap and wedged his own knife into the end. "Ready?"

"Ready." It was an old ritual by now. Together, they twisted their knives to pry the oysters open. Tug always had an easier time of it; his short, stubby fingers were made for grasping and manipulating objects, while Koa's were really only for flight and climbing. Still, by now, he was used to it. He tugged the split shell of the oyster open. White flesh stretched apart.

"Anything?" Tug asked.

Koa prodded at the flesh with a claw. "Nope." He handed the oyster to Tug, who sucked the shells clean.

Koa shuddered. "I don't know how you can stand those." Even the smell upon opening the shells was awful—musty and fishy.

"Delicious." Tug smacked his lips. "You're missing out, Breezy."

"Yuck. Give me another." He took the next oyster, waited for Tug, opened that one, and then together they opened the next two. Nothing.

Tug took the last one. "This has to be the one. It's our day for it. We nearly got eaten. And you… you nearly drowned."

"I did not." Koa stuck out his tongue.

"*Nearly drowned.* So I figure this is our time. The universe owes us a pearl."

"A big one."

"Size of my fist. That's why I saved this fella for last." Tug hefted an admittedly huge oyster into his lap and patted its shell.

"Fist, nothing. That's got to have one the size of your head."

"Size of my head, and pink as sunrise. Valuable enough to buy you and me and the family a whole Arm."

Koa grinned. "All the Arms."

"Valuable enough to buy us a whole Kingdom. And we'll all go and live there and we'll stay wherever we want—Knees, Belly,

Shoulders, even the Crown. And there won't be any stuffy old bats either."

"Except me," Koa pointed out.

"Pfah, you're no bat. You're an otter. Honorary, anyway, which is just as good. Well. Half as good. One tenth."

Koa lobbed a dollop of mud at Tug, and it landed on the side of his face with a satisfying splat. "Just shut up and open the mudding oyster, already, you soggy lowlife."

Tug grinned, wiping the mud away with the back of one paw. "I take it back, you *are* a bat, you stuck-up airhead." He worked the end of his knife into the oyster, gave it a firm twist, and pried it apart with his claws. He stared down at the shells.

"Well?" Koa demanded, after Tug said nothing.

He shook his head in mock sadness. "I'm afraid the universe didn't like that ugly slur toward otters, and has taken back our pearl."

Koa flopped backward onto the floor, spreading his shredded wings. "Because why should today be any different than any other day."

The otter squinted at him. "Well, there is *one* thing that might make it a bit different." He patted around his clothes as though rummaging for a misplaced purse. "Now where's it gone?"

Koa opened one eye. "You're a wretched actor, you know that, don't you?"

"Am I?" Tug asked innocently. "Well then, how'd I manage to get this late in the day without you working out that I'd had *this* the whole time?" He opened his webbed fingers to reveal a thin metal necklace of twining silver fashioned around small turquoise gems. The silver was somewhat tarnished by the salt water, but the turquoise was still bright blue. He grinned at Koa's dumbfounded expression. "This is it, isn't it? I can just throw it back if you—"

"Yes, yes, that's certainly it!" Koa snatched the necklace from Tug's hand and held it up to the light. "I can't believe you found it."

"I know, it's an awfully huge accomplishment, finding something water-colored in water. So careless of him to lose it."

"Him!" Koa hopped to his feet. "We have to go take it to him now! He's going to be so amazed."

"Well, go give it to him."

"You're coming too. You have to. You found it, after all."

"And was very nearly poo for it," Tug agreed. "Course I'm coming with you. If I head home, Mum's likely to get the idea that I can be useful, and put it to experimentation. Better a moony-eyed bat than paws full of urchin needles, eh?"

Chapter 3

The community improvement projects were in the Belly of the Kingdom of Beards, one tree away from Titan. To get to it, Koa had to climb all the way up to one of the Arms, follow it to the end, and take the Canting Bridge to the Beards.

The bridge itself was long and sagging, stretching nearly a quarter of a mile between the trees. It swayed even in low breezes, which was how it got its name. Koa thought its construction rather poor, but then, it was held together and supported by magic spells inscribed on every slat and rope. It was strung high so that the seawater wouldn't douse the magic, but now and then a large storm would carry the spray of the waves so far up that the bridge would collapse. This had only happened twice in his life—once during the Great Storm, and once about five years ago. That time he'd worked to help fix it, and nearly every solid knot or well-chosen strand remaining on the bridge he could claim to his own credit.

That didn't stop Tug from whinging about the crossing every single time they made it.

"I don't see why we can't just take a boat," he moaned about halfway across, clinging with both arms to the guide rope as the wind blew the bridge nearly sideways.

"You've got money for the docking fee all of a sudden? I don't see what you're worried about. It's just water down there."

"Oi, about five hundred feet down! It wouldn't be like falling into a lovely bed of rose petals. I'd splatter across it like a rotten persimmon. And that's *if* I didn't get stuck through on one of the Toes and paint it red with my gizzards."

"Otters haven't got gizzards, so logically you'd be fine." Koa didn't mind the bridge so much. Though he'd never survive a fall, he could grip each plank with his feet and feel completely secure, and even fruit bats who *could* fly were accustomed to climbing about. Besides, the spells were solid. It took a measure of determination to fall from the Canting Bridge. "You know," he added, "you don't have to come along *every* time."

Tug gritted his teeth through a particularly strong gust of wind that sent the bridge creaking. "What, you think you're the only one that can go romanticating? There are girls there too, you know."

"Bat girls," Koa reminded him.

"Right, so there's no worry about shiny things on fingers later, or squalling babes to anchor you. They just want a bit of fun with a rustic otter bloke. Or ain't you heard of toelickers?"

"You're disgusting."

"And proud of it, little brother."

Koa reached the end and helped Tug to solid bark—as usual, once the otter had his feet under him, he acted like nothing had ever disconcerted him.

The Beards was named for the great curtains of shaggy, grey moss that hung from every branch. On evenings like this, cool clouds of sea fog blew in and clustered among the limbs, shrouding the tree. As the evening deepened, the fog illuminated with the pale white, red, or gold of glowlamps blooming to life all through the great tree, shifting or pulsing as the breeze swayed the moss. Koa always loved the sight of it.

He had no time to stare now, though. He led Tug down winding paths and ladders, descending from the Shoulders to the Belly, where the Beards' trunk broadened and split with hollows and crevices where families nestled their homes, where vendors set up shops to sell coffee or frozen mangos or roasted nuts to those on their way back and forth between home and work or shopping or entertainment.

The flying foxes had already clustered on one of the lower branches, nearly all of them young, in their late teens or early twenties. They had settled around a somewhat elderly bat, one so paunchy that Koa wondered he could fly at all.

Koa crept closer, hunching low so as not to be seen, and ducked behind a large branch, peering out from behind. Tug sauntered up behind him and leaned on the branch, watching with casual interest.

The elderly bat stood in the midst of the circle of younger bats, fussing with a little notebook, and as the chatter died down, he looked up and announced, "Welcome, students. As you know if you've been consulting your syllabus, today for community projects we begin footway maintenance."

A few grumbles went around the crowd of students, and the elderly fox nodded. "Yes, I know some of you may wonder about the importance of the footways. Perhaps you think them little more than an afterthought, grudgingly installed for those who live below. But it is easy to forget how advantaged we are with our power of flight. Those without it rely on the footways for their lives and livelihoods. Remember, the tallest trees are still only as mighty as their roots. It is our responsibility to cultivate them—not only the roots of our home, but the roots of our society as well. To remind you all what the less fortunate must face every day, none of you will be permitted to fly for the duration."

This time the grumbling was louder and angrier.

"Yes, by the time you've finished, you will appreciate the true privilege of flight, and how meaningful that capability is. Your group leaders have been given your assignments, so flap to it. Or ought I say, climb to it?" He chuckled, but no one chuckled with him.

Tug leaned over to Koa. "Windy old mashbag, ain't he? Good of him to feel so sorry for us footy types what have to crawl around like bugs."

Koa shrugged. "He cares. That's more than you can say for a lot of bats."

"Speaking of a lot of bats, I don't see yours. He not show today?"

"No, he's down there." Koa pointed a wing toward one of the young bats—tall, slender, with wide round glasses and reddish-blond fur that poofed out around his ears. "See? Come on, you know him. The handsome one."

"Aw, they all look alike to me. Folded up dishtowels with fox faces, every one. And look at them horrible feets. No webs at all."

Koa ignored him, watching the handsome one conferring with his fellow students. "His name is Maiel. His father—"

"I know *that* part. His dad's a big muckety-muck wizard who makes the spells that protect the Kingdom, and *he's* deep in his books to be a boring old lawyer which for some reason you think is great. You ain't exactly keeping secrets about your future splash-in-the-wake. But how do you know he fancies the boys?"

"He had a boyfriend before. But then they fought, and now he's—oh no, the professor's got them working on the ladders!" Koa winced, watching the students pull long coils of rope out of nearby sacks and begin clustering around some of the older rope ladders, picking at water-tightened knots.

Tug punched his shoulder. "Don't worry, little brother. I'm sure they read all about it in books. They'll do it up right for once."

Koa covered his face with one wing.

"So when you gonna give him back his necklace, huh? Or you just planning to just toss it into his pocket when he ain't looking?"

"I dunno," Koa said, backing up behind the branch. "He's not going to want to talk to me. He's all educated and refined, and—"

"Well, so are you! You read all those books to yourself when you ought to be out fishing and playing kickball and such. And you're—well, not refined, but *fined*, anyway. Remember when you stole the boatmaster's brandy?"

Koa rolled his eyes. "It wasn't brandy. It was *cognac*. And—"

"See? Refined. So go and give him his little jewelry thing back and have a flirt with him!"

"I can't just walk up to him out of nowhere. It'd be weird."

"Right, because secretly watching someone for a month from a hidden place is much more normal." Tug leaned out from behind the branch, craning his neck. "He's jauntin' this way now. Go on!"

The thought burned at Koa's ears. Maiel was used to the upper world, one of gentility and manners and delicacy. Most books Koa had read were set in that world—stories of courtly intrigue, secret enchantments and political machinations. There weren't kings or princes anymore, but Maiel practically was one, the son of a high wizard, raised in wealth and high society, with the very best schooling and tutelage available.

Koa was intensely aware of his own shortcomings. His education was meager, his manners rude. He had no money for fur conditioners or stylists or tailors. His mother had made the clothes he wore now—a rough shirt, pinned to the canvas shorts so that it wouldn't fall over his head when he hung upside down. He would look like a yokel standing next to Maiel, who wore a red velvet vest with gold buttons and a puffy shirt, which looped around his wings and was held in place by enchantments. And *that* was his outfit for working on ladders.

Above all, Koa dreaded the look on Maiel's face upon seeing his shredded wings. They were a disfigurement he did his best to hide, keeping his arms folded to his side when around other bats. When he was younger, he had tried fixing the torn flaps of skin together with globs of sticky mangrove sap, but they had not held, and had picked up so much other debris that others had burst out laughing when they saw him. Laughter was even worse than the usual looks of pity and disgust—or sometimes outright horror—that other bats gave him if they saw his wings. The thought of that expression on Maiel's handsome muzzle was too much to bear.

He shook his head. "Not today. Maybe—maybe tomorrow, if I get cleaned up."

Tug looked down, scuffing one paw against the bark. "I'm real sorry to hear you say that, little brother."

Koa shrugged. "Well, it's not like you—"

"Because that means that you're gonna be mad as blazes at me for doin' *this!*" Tug gave him a hard shove on the chest.

Koa flailed his wings, stumbling backward from behind the branch. Nearly, he fell over, but he spun around, lurched to the side, and caught his balance.

"Oh!" said a voice right in front of him.

He blinked, finding himself chest to chest with Maiel. Well, chest to nose—the flying fox was shorter than him by a head. He smelled like persimmon and spices, and for only a second, Koa forgot himself. His fur prickled with electric excitement. Then, horrified, he scrambled backward. "I'm so, so sorry," he said. "Sir," he added, remembering Maiel's station.

"Oh no, please." Maiel looked amused rather than offended, his ears forward. "This is *your* part of the tree, after all. Not mine."

The aristocracy of Koa's books had a special talent for nesting subtle insult within compliments, but Koa didn't need an education to tell him the hidden meaning there: I don't belong down here. You do. His cheeks burned. "But you have a class here right now. I didn't mean to get in your way." He held his wings close to his sides so that Maiel wouldn't see their rents. "I—I need to get going."

"Just a moment," Maiel said as he turned to go. "You're that climbing bat, aren't you? The laddermaker, I mean."

Koa looked back. "I'm named Koa, if it please you." The bat giggled at him, and he realized he'd said something foolish just then. People said "If it please you" in the stories, but he should have known modern-day flying foxes wouldn't talk that way. He cursed Tug for pushing him out here. He should have let the croc eat him. "I mean, yes sir, I'm the laddermaker."

"Fantastic. But please don't call me sir. I am Maiel, of the Crown of the Bearded Kingdom." He gave a little bow. "I do hope we aren't taking your job from you, what with all the repairs we're doing tonight. I'd hate to think we were depriving you of a little coin."

Koa glanced over Maiel's shoulder at the other bats. Plainly none of them had ever worked with any rope sturdier than a curtain cord. Many of them were tying the wrong knots entirely, and those who had got it right were still working their loops loosely, or unbalanced. His ears went back. "No. No, I think there will still be… plenty of work for me."

"Ah, wonderful." Maiel put a wing to his mouth, catching his breath. "I mean, not wonderful, if you have *too* much work to do, and you never get rest. It's a pity the way some laborers are worked nearly to death, don't you think?"

"Er, I suppose? Everyone I know gets by all right."

Maiel nodded soberly. "We all know what you do, of course, keeping the pathways safe, the ladders strong, and the Crown connected to the Toes. It must be so hard for you."

Koa blinked at him.

"I mean, with your—" Maiel waved one wing toward Koa. "You know."

Koa drew his wings in closer. "You mean because I can't fly." Were his scars showing? Were his torn strips of numb flesh fluttering in the breeze?

"Well… yes. It's just that I think you must be very courageous."

"Courageous? Why?"

"Well—well, you—" Maiel took a step back, looking flustered. "I mean, that—that thing happened to you, and you lost your—your home, I mean, and you can't fly, but you still come out every day and you work, and you live a normal life as… as best as you can. You know? And that takes courage."

Koa flushed. "Oh. Because someone like me should be afraid? Of coming out every day and living a normal life?"

A *hssst* sound came from behind the branch. He looked over and saw Tug with his webbed paws up, shaking his head and mouthing *noooooo* at him. He cringed. He hadn't meant his words to sound so confrontational, but everything kept coming out of his muzzle wrong.

Maiel frowned. "That wasn't what I meant. Or maybe—I don't know. I'm sorry. I didn't mean to bother you." He turned.

Fighting a rising panic at how badly everything was going, Koa shouted, "Wait!"

The little bat turned back to him with a questioning expression.

"I came up here because about a month ago you were doing community projects on Titan."

"Yes, I remember," Maiel said, looking cautious.

"And something fell from around your neck."

"Ah. You noticed that? Yes, it was a necklace of mine. My mother's, actually. Ensorcelled not to fall, but you know, one splash of seawater, and—"

"Is this it?" Koa's pocket was lined with little hooks to keep him from losing things as he climbed or hung from the Kingdoms. He unclipped the necklace from one of these hooks and held it out to Maiel.

The little bat blinked, his large ears perked high. "How remarkable. It looks just like it. But it can't be."

"I saw where it went. My brother and I fished it out. I'd hoped to find it sooner, but—"

"Your brother?"

Tug stuck a whiskered face out from behind the branch. "Hullo. I, er, ain't spyin'. Here on totally separate business. Him. He's the spyin' one."

Koa flinched, but Maiel didn't frown or scowl. Instead he folded his wings and made a little bow. "I am indebted to you both. This is truly astonishing. I had never expected to see this again. You've no idea how deeply I felt its loss." He straightened and looked back and forth between Tug and Koa. "You must allow me to show my gratitude."

Koa felt the heat rise to his face. "I really couldn't accept—"

"—A punch in the face," Tug supplied helpfully. "Money would be just fine, but he gets awful shirty about being knocked in the gob. So don't do that, whatever."

Koa shoved him back behind the branch again. "I'm never inviting you along again."

"I'll take it under advisement," Maiel said with a smile. He paused as if considering something, and took a deep breath. "Listen, I don't suppose you've ever been to a Firefly Ball, but you must have heard of them."

Koa certainly had—everyone had. The Firefly Balls were weekly parties, always thrown in the Crown of one Kingdom or another, in the upper reaches where only bats could go. Naturally, no one he knew had ever been to one—even if you could climb or fly up into the branches, enchantments kept out anyone but flying foxes. Climb high enough, and a tangible but invisible barrier would slow you down until you could ascend no farther. Naturally, everyone was insatiably curious about the parties, and everyone claimed a story or two of their own. One wallaby who ran an inn in the Shoulders of the Great Drinker had a telescope, and whenever the Firefly Ball came to the adjacent Kingdoms, he would charge people fifty rupiah to look through it and make out any details they could. People had stories of strange fruits piled high or carved into humorous shapes, of dancing lights and colored smoke and fantastical costumes.

Koa had actually been to several of the balls, but that had been long ago, before the Great Storm, when he was just a pup, and whatever true memories he had of those parties were now inextricably mingled with the tales he had heard since. He remembered them being exciting, but scary—adult events, filled with tall bats who were interested in dancing or talking with each other and not in indulging tagalong pups. Images flickered through his mind: an exotic and strangely alluring male dressed in deep, elegant purples, with odd silver jewels that didn't fall off even when upside down; a scary-looking female bat dressed in sparkling green who had leaned down to huff her nose-stinging breath in his face as she gushed about how precious he was. He'd cried for his mother after that.

It was easier to lie. "No, I've never been to one. I've always been curious."

"There is one tomorrow night, you know. Here in the Beards." Maiel looked him up and down. "You should come. You're invited, of course. You're a flying fox. You're invited to all of them."

Koa realized his jaw was hanging open like a yokel's and snapped it closed. "But I'm—" He looked down at himself and shrugged.

Maiel stepped closer and put his wing on Koa's shoulder. "Courageous," he said. His breath was sweet honey.

A little tickle of cool wind crawled over Koa's shoulder and down his spine. He stared into the smaller bat's chestnut brown eyes and forgot how to breathe. "Yeah," he said.

"So what's all this, then?" a loud and officious voice demanded. "Is this one bothering you, Maiel?"

Koa recognized the owner of the voice as Hayden, a tall and thin bat with purple-tinged fur. Hayden ostensibly worked in their community projects as well, but Koa had noticed he much preferred to follow other bats around and make corrective comments about their own tasks.

Maiel drew himself up taller as though he had suddenly remembered his station. "No, of course not. Hayden, this is the worker who maintains many of our bridges and ladders."

"Many of *their* bridges and ladders, you mean," Hayden sniffed. "It isn't as though we require them." He looked Koa up and down the same way he might eye an overripe banana. "You know, if you attended your tasks a shade more closely, perhaps your betters wouldn't be out here fixing up your work."

Koa gritted his teeth and reminded himself that he had no right to argue. "Time, strain, and weather will break even the strongest ropes, sir."

"Sir. Do you hear that?" Hayden nudged Maiel with a wing. "He knows his place well enough, doesn't he?"

"His place is with us," Maiel answered, before Koa could say anything. "You remember the Great Storm. He had no relatives to take him in."

"No, but he has some now, hasn't he?" Hayden said. "You *were* taken in, weren't you, boy? You've got a delightful little home down in the Toes."

"Yes, sir."

Hayden grinned nastily. "A whole warren of wriggling swamp rats, I heard."

Koa fought a sudden urge to lunge at him. "Otters." He purposefully left off the sir this time. "But you could be forgiven for the mistake. Your education can't be too concerned with the lower classes. Not if that rope work is any indication. But I suppose the upper classes can't be bothered with honest work."

Hayden's supercilious smile faded. Koa felt a moment of satisfaction, and then saw Maiel's dismayed expression and knew he'd gone too far. Hayden swallowed as though he'd bitten into something sour and didn't want to spit it out, but then relaxed, letting the smile flow back over his face again. "Oh, how *desperately* tragic," he crooned. "You think your little jobs are vital. You think it's honest work! Maiel, isn't that positively heartbreaking? The little mud-dweller toils night and day just to make his little bridges and ladders, and why? Just so that he and his fellows can climb a little higher, to try to get a taste of the world they lost. They think if they can just reach the top of the Kingdom, they'll be like us."

Maiel stepped in between them, lifting his wings. "Stop it, Hayden. You're being rude."

Koa barely heard him. Blood pounded in his ears. He stepped forward, past Maiel, baring his teeth.

Hayden ignored his threatening pose. "But you'll never be anything like us. Do you know why?" He leaned forward and hissed the words in apparent delight. "Because you can't fly. And nothing you do will ever change that."

Anger and shame thrummed through Koa. "At least I know how to treat other people decently," he shouted, and he lifted his wing to give Hayden a shove on the chest, but the purple-furred bat caught Koa's wing in his own and, before Koa could stop him, pulled it out to its full span.

"By the Twelve Gods," he breathed. "It's *disgusting*."

Koa stood in horror, his wing outstretched. He didn't look down at it. He knew what the other bats saw: a shredded mass of gnarled flesh and misshapen bone. The skin was white and brown—black in places, with a snarl of white and reddish scar tissue that bulged out like lumps of rope beneath the skin. His long wing-fingers were skewed, and one of them jutted forward like a twisted tooth. In between, the sails were torn from tip to arm, long strips dangling and fluttering in the wind, loose ribbons of flesh.

"Oh, Koa," came Maiel's voice. It was full of pity and, Koa thought, revulsion.

"Here now." That was Tug, coming back out from behind the branch, putting his paws on Koa's shoulders. "I think we'd better go. We've already had our share of nasty-toothed things today, haven't we?"

Koa wrenched his wing away, ɔurning with shame. "Leave me alone!" He pulled his wings tightly to his side. Then he saw beyond the purple-furred bat. Behind him, the whole class was staring, their eyes round. Some wore expressions of disgust. Others laughed. Most looked shocked.

And on Maiel's face, he saw the twisted expression of repulsion and loathing, contorting his handsome features. "Hayden, how could you?" Maiel began, but Koa didn't wait to listen. He fled. And he fled awkwardly, crawling as fast as he could on foot and wing, because he could not fly.

Chapter 4

Koa poked at his sliced persimmon with a fork. He didn't feel much like eating. A heaviness settled across him like a giant wet blanket. It's always been there, pressing me down, he thought to himself. And I'm just getting too tired to stand up tall anymore.

"Oi, Koa! The chilies!"

"What?" He looked up from his plate. His oldest brother, Demel, waved a huge webbed paw at him.

"You gone to sleep? Toss the chilies down this way!"

Flanked by a long bench on each side, the family dining table was enormous—it had to be, to seat Koa, his eight brothers, four sisters, mother, father, and whatever guests they might have. It had started out only six feet long, but as the family grew, so had the table, with addition after addition nailed to it, until Koa's father had had to chop out the eastern wall and expand the size of their home. Koa usually sat at the far end, the clamor of twelve energetic otter siblings often proving too much for him. Like tonight. He sighed and passed the bowl of chilies to Eliva, who passed it to Mak, who passed it to Tug, who passed it to Syrus, who passed it to Demel.

"Cheers." Demel blanketed his fish and rice with a layer of the green chilies.

Koa wrinkled his muzzle. He didn't mind the heavy scents of spice and fish that filled the kitchen. They smelled like home.

They were comforting. But at the same time, they were so obtrusive and powerful that they drowned everything else out. He preferred food with delicate flavors and scents that evolved and bloomed in his nose as he chewed. But he could only truly enjoy them away from home; here, they just tasted sweet and tart and a little fishy.

"Aren't you hungry?" Eliva asked with evinced concern. She had been acting motherly lately, despite being two years younger than him. Koa guessed it had something to do with her boyfriend, who was always talking about pups and how important parenting was.

"Not really," Koa said. "Guess I'm just tired."

"Tired of getting made fun of." That was Syrus, crossing his thin arms and leaning over to eye everyone meaningfully. "My watchman friend said he was hanging around those university bats again, and there was a scuffle."

The four or five loud conversations going on all up and down the table hushed.

"What? What'd he say?"

"He said Koa was almost in a fight with other bats."

Syrus snorted. "Yeah, right, like Koa would fight anyone. It was Tug. He went swinging at some stuck-up rich boy after Koa got picked on again."

Koa peered down the table at Tug, who shrugged.

"Bet you almost pissed yourself holding onto that mudding announcement, Syrus," said Demel.

"Demel!" Their mother stood and put both paws on the table, frowning. "Not at the table."

"Sorry," Demel said, plainly not sorry.

"Syrus, you know I don't like gossip."

"Sorry," Syrus said, even more unapologetic than Demel.

"Good." Their mother sat down and cut into her fish, chewing a moment. "So, a fight?"

"Weren't a fight," Tug muttered into his plate. "Syrus is makin' a big deal out of nothin'."

"It better not be," their father said, looking up over his glasses. "We don't fight in this family."

Teel, Koa's youngest sister, stuck up a stubby paw. "Um. Um."

"Yes, Teel?" their mother asked.

"Today Mak hit Ruko in the arm with a potato."

"Ugh, shut up, Teel," Mak groaned.

"Shut up is a rude thing to say," she informed him severely.

Koa hunched down in his chair and hoped the commotion would take over any attempt at conversation, as usual.

"It's not an exaggeration!" Syrus's words pierced the commotion. It wasn't too big an achievement for him—he was gifted with what their mother affectionately referred to as a preacher's voice. "My friend said he thought he was going to have to step in. He said Tug went wild, just started haulin' off at this other bat. Popped him in the jaw twice. Two other bats had to pull him off."

Koa sunk lower in his seat. He hadn't heard this. He'd heard shouting after he'd run off, but he hadn't thought Tug would go after the guy.

Syrus sat taller, practically vibrating with righteousness. "He told me it's lucky for us that the bat didn't want to press charges. He could have had Tug spell-bound for a week."

Their father put down his fork. He stared at Tug, his bush of whiskers twitching.

"Aww, you done it now, Tug," Mak crowed.

"Mak, if it isn't your tail, don't wag it," their mother said around a mouthful of fish.

"All right, Tug," their father said. "Let's hear the good explanation I know you have."

The words exploded from Tug's muzzle like they'd been building pressure in there. "It's not my fault! I had to! You don't understand! If you'd been there, if you'd seen what they did to Koa—"

"Did they attack him?"

Don't tell them, Koa mentally beseeched Tug. *They don't need to know how humiliating it was. They don't need to know how I ran away. How stupid I was talking to Maiel.* He wished he could meet Tug's eyes—a look would be enough to keep him quiet about it—but Tug was focused on their father.

"Well, sort of. They didn't knock him around, but look, why do you think that twit don't wanna drag me before a judge? It's because he don't want all them uppy-ups knowing how he picked on a crip—"

He faltered. The room was quiet. He looked down the table toward Koa with a miserable expression. Koa stared down at the persimmon, untouched, on his plate.

Tug hit the table with one fist. "Come on, you know I don't think that way! But *they* do. They think that way about all of us. And then that one grabbed his wing and pulled it out and said nasty things, and then Koa scarpered, and you could see he was hurt, and I—I *had* to hit him, didn't I? I was full o' violence and I had to get it out of me or go blind."

"You. Are so. Insane."

"Shut up, Mak," Demel said.

Their mother brushed at her whiskers with both paws. "I don't understand. I thought the university students were working over in the Beards. What were you doing over there?" Tug went quiet, settling back onto the bench. She looked at him, and then down the table. "Koa?"

Koa tried to make his shrug look nonchalant. "Just… curious."

"Yeah, curious about getting laid," Syrus sneered. "He's been over there for weeks watching some little bat boy he likes."

Koa's face burned. He briefly envisioned Syrus tumbling from Titan's Crown all the way down to the Toes and hitting every branch on the way down.

Teel stuck up her paw. "Um. Koa likes boys and not girls."

"Yes, Teel," their mother said.

"But most boys like girls and not boys."

"Thank you, Teel. Koa, you know I don't think it's healthy to be following those bats around. I know you're interested in them, but—well, they're from Heads and Crowns."

"So am I," he muttered.

She sighed. "I know you are, honey, but you live here, with us, and they… people like that don't really understand people like us. They'll hurt you without meaning to."

"Or *because* they mean to," Tug growled.

Koa braced both his wings on the edge of table. "Well, what am I supposed to do, mom? People like that? I *am* people like that. I'm supposed to be up there. I'm a bat, mom. You think I'm going to go find a nice otter and settle down?"

His father frowned, his thick bristle of whiskers drooping. "Koa, calm down when you talk to your mother."

"Honey, I just don't want to see you get hurt," his mother said.

"Well I *am* hurt!" Koa shouted. He stood up from the table and spread his wings, letting the ragged strips dangle. "You think anything can hurt me more than this?"

She didn't look down, keeping her eyes on his. "That never used to matter to you."

"Well it matters now. How many guys out there could love this?"

"Um, four and a half," Teel hazarded. Mak and Ruko snickered into their paws.

Koa ignored them. "If I have any chance at all, *any* chance, I have to take it. And I can't worry about being hurt. The rest of you, you all get to take your time. You get to pick and choose. But not me. Because I'm broken. This boy is nice. He's sweet and gentle. Maybe he's my one chance. And if I have to be around a bunch of rich snots to be with him, then that's what I have to do. And anyone who's trying to stop me from taking that one chance is not helping me."

He turned to storm out, which was awkward, because he had to stalk all the way down the full length of the table, squeezing past chairs that were pushed out too far, and tripping over his sister's bag, so by the time he reached the door, he was even more flushed and angry than before. So he turned to Tug and snapped, "And I don't need anyone else fighting my battles for me. You don't have to come with me anymore."

Then he left, stepping out into the muggy night air, thinking of the wounded look on Tug's face. It was satisfying for about ten seconds, and then he just felt guilty and awful, and wanted to run back inside and apologize, but that would be worse.

Their home was nestled in the crook between two of Titan's wide Toes, and a path down one of these led to the family docks, where their boats were tied off. It was no good taking one of those out. His wings were useless for rowing.

Instead, he followed the Toe upward, climbing past the walls of the house, and hopped over onto the roof. He sprawled out, spreading his wings across the cool clay tiles. When he lay in just the right spot, he could see past the slope of the trunk, higher and higher, past all of Titan's great spreading Arms, past the series of Nets that prevented dropped objects from tumbling all the way to the Toes, up to the Crown. The world he had fallen from was brilliantly lit, glowing with reds and yellows. The lights above shifted and swayed. And sometimes, even down here, thousands of feet below, when the commotion from his home stilled and the waves of the swamp-sea quieted, he thought he could hear the faint strains of music and laughter.

And the front door opening.

"Koa?" It was his father's voice.

He sighed, not wanting to answer, not wanting the talk that he knew was coming. But he'd been enough of a jerk for one night. "Yeah. I'm up here."

A series of grunts came from below as his father clambered up to the roof. "Ugh." His father rubbed at his shoulder. "The house gets taller every year, I swear." He peered in Koa's direction. "It's so dark. You haven't lit your glowlamp."

"I don't need it, Dad," Koa began, but his father was already moving toward the edge of the roof, reaching over to touch a large, round globe that swung from an old rope. At his touch, cool white light welled up inside it, glowing so brightly that it dimmed Koa's view of the lights above. The globe revolved at the end of its rope, and each time it turned toward Koa, he could see the shape carved into its side—that of a smiling flying fox, its wings spread, shining like a beacon.

"You used to love this thing," his father said, paws on his hips as he gazed at it. "Fifteen years it's been lighting. Most of these things burn out after—"

"After ten, I know. But some last twenty or more. It's not that weird, Dad."

"You should light it when you come out."

"I'm not a kid anymore. I don't need a nightlight. I have better night vision than you."

"Yeah. I guess you're not." His father made his way across the roof, his paws making little *pat-pat* sounds against the tiles. He sat down next to Koa, and leaned over to look up with him at the soft lights above. "Anything happening up there?"

"How would I know?"

His father shrugged. "I guess I don't know too much about where you go or what you do these days. I didn't know you'd found a friend."

"He's not a friend, he's just—I like him. We've barely spoken. And maybe he won't want to, now. He invited me to the Firefly Ball."

His father was quiet for a minute. "Are you going to go?"

"Like this?" Koa flapped his ragged wings against the roof.

"They were cruel to you, weren't they?"

Koa said nothing, but the promise of tears formed at the corners of his eyes. He concentrated until they went away.

When his father spoke again, his voice was soft and distant, and he looked out over the swamp-sea. "That night of the Great Storm, the wind was so high, we thought it must be the end of the world. Titan swayed like a cattail. Houses fell apart, and things began tumbling from the branches. A stove from up in the Head fell right down through our roof—did I ever tell you that? Smashed right through the roof into the den. We're lucky it didn't kill anyone."

"You told me," Koa sighed.

"And your mother and I figured the place wasn't safe, and we'd better get the pups out before the whole roof came down. We all went outside—there were only seven of us then—and we all kept low so that the wind wouldn't take us right off the Toes and into the sea. The waves were bad. I told your mother we had to climb higher, but then we saw Atlas. There was so much water in the air we could hardly make it out. Just a silhouette. But then your mother screamed and pointed, and I saw one of the Arms just tearing away like a leaf. Then the whole thing started to fall. It was unbelievable. Your brothers and sisters were crying, and the roots were coming up and then it just went over. Like the whole world was falling. And I told your mother, we've got to get higher, there's going to be a mudding wave like you've never seen. So we tried, but the ladders weren't any good in the storm, whipping all around.

"We didn't even see the wave before it hit. One minute we were trying to crawl up the Toes, the next we were underwater, not knowing which direction was up. Thank the Twelve that all the pups had learned to swim. And that none of them got smashed into debris." He breathed out slowly.

Koa remembered nothing of that night, but he had heard the story so many times, picturing it in his mind, that the memories seemed like his own. "And then a boat drifted by," he prompted his father.

"Yes, still whole, somehow. Not ours—those were both smashed to bits. I think this one actually came from Atlas. But anyway, the storm died down pretty soon after Atlas fell. There were still waves, but not as bad. So I started rowing around, calling for your mother and your brothers and sisters, and meanwhile it's like there was never a storm at all—the sky is clear, and there are stars—but I can hear all these people above crying and screaming. And all this stuff floating in the water. Bodies, too." Koa pricked his ears. He hadn't heard that part of the story before. "Each time I saw one, I was so afraid it might be one of the pups, or your mother, I thought my heart was going to squeeze down into a little cold rock. But then I heard your mother calling back to me. She'd found Demel and Syrus and Lissie on her own, no boat or anything. And then we found the rest and took them back to one of the Toes, and I told your mother, I've got to go back out there, there might be others who need help. And Demel and Syrus came too, and we went toward Atlas, just calling out for anyone who might answer back.

"It was grim. We didn't hear anyone calling back. And Atlas was lying half-sunk in the water, most of its Arms broken, wrecked houses and boats everywhere. And underwater, you could see all those glowlamps, still shining, way down deep. The seawater hadn't got into 'em yet, I guess. There was nothing left. Most of the bats got blown off, those that could get away. Everyone else..." He shook his head.

"Syrus was the one who heard you. He said, 'Go that way, Dad, I hear someone crying.' I ever tell you that part?"

Koa snorted. "Yeah. And even if you didn't, he reminds me every chance he gets."

"If it wasn't for him, we might not have found you. You were pinned up in this big snarl of broken wood, your wings all twisted, branches going through them. I didn't know. I said, son, I'm sorry, but I'm not sure we can save this little guy. You were pretty torn up, just crying your head off. And he said, 'You have to, Dad, you have to save him.' So we pulled you off the branches as best as we could—"

"And you put me in the boat and came back and got me bandaged up and took me in," Koa finished for him. "You know I'm grateful, Dad. I really am. I never felt like I wasn't family, ever."

"Well, I appreciate that. But there's something I never told you. When we put you down in the boat, you didn't stay. You squirmed up and hopped right over the edge back into the water. You just kind of flailed there, splashing, and Demel jumped out and got you and put you back in the boat. But as soon as he let go, you jumped out into the water again."

Koa sat up, looking at his father, puzzled. "Why would I do that? Was I scared of you or something?"

"Well, that's what I wondered, too, but then Syrus said you were looking at the lights. And sure enough, when we pulled you out again, and held you, you just kept staring down at those glowlamps under the water, reaching your little broken wings out to them. I think you thought that's where your parents were, down there with the lights. And you were just trying to get back to them."

He looked down and patted Koa's arm. "When I told your mother about that, she picked you up and wouldn't let you go for anything. Then a few days later she came home with that glowlamp. Carved a little fruit bat into the side and hung it outside. When I asked her why, she said it was so you'd always know where home was."

Koa said nothing, but he glanced over at the glowlamp and guilt plucked at him.

His father leaned back on the roof and looked up through the Arms of Titan, where the Crown shifted and danced with warm light. "We would have sent you back with your family if we could, but they were all gone with the storm. From then on, we never thought of you as anything but a son. I guess I knew that you wouldn't want an otter's life forever. I thought you'd find a good one with us. But here you are, still staring after those lights, still reaching for them."

"I can't stop wanting to see that world," Koa answered. "Those are my people up there. I have to know what it's like. I have to find someone else like me. Those lights—you can't stop me from reaching for them."

"I know that, son." His father rolled awkwardly to his feet with a grunt, and made his way to the edge of the roof. He looked back. "I guess sometimes I'm just still afraid you're going to drown."

Chapter 5

The next day, after another unsuccessful fishing trip, Koa and Tug lugged a couple bags of salvage into a boat and rowed over to the Kingdom of the Great Drinker, a wide-trunked, bulbous mangrove whose trunk was hollow. Channels had been carefully carved into all of its Arms and they continually flowed with rain and dew that collected in its upper branches. The waters ran down, splashing and pouring, until they drained into the great, thirsty belly of the tree, forming the Drink, a deep pool of fresh water for the use of all the Kingdoms.

Tug moored the boat at an uncle's dock and they both climbed up the winding paths of the Drinker, past the Toes and Knees until they reached the Belly. The swell of it loomed over them, and the resonant wood amplified the sound of the water pouring and splashing into the lake above. It was here, below the bulge of the Belly, that the hedge lizard lived and purveyed his enchanted goods, "right in the crotch," as Tug was fond of putting it. The shop was hollowed into a giant gnarl, and its walls vibrated continually with the movements of the Drink.

Koa had been in a black mood all morning. In one pocket he thumbed at the letter that had arrived for him that morning. A young messenger bat had come to the door, handed it to him, dipped his cap, and flown off again. The paper had been fine, the lettering calligraphic. He had never seen his own name written so elegantly before. He'd climbed up on the roof to read it, afraid even to open it.

> *Dear Koa,*
>
> *It is my sad obligation to notify you that, in light of recent events, I think it best to rescind my invitation to the Firefly Ball. Please understand that I hold you in no less regard after the regrettable events of yesterday, and offer my humble sympathies for any harm done to you; however, it would seem pursuing any further association at this time would be unwise. I do hope you understand.*
>
> *Yours, Maiel of the Crown of the Bearded Kingdom*

So that was it. His once chance, gone. He'd read and reread the letter, searching for any sign of hope. *At this time*—so perhaps another time might be acceptable? But no, it was all just typical upper-Crown politeness. It meant nothing. Maiel had seen what he was and wanted nothing more to do with him. It was all he should have expected. He'd been glad for the chance to go fishing—something to take his mind off the letter for a while—and Tug had seen that he wasn't in the mood to talk, and hadn't pressed him.

But now, as they climbed the rope ladder to the hedge lizard's shop, the heavy bag of salvage strapped over his wings, Tug finally spoke up. "Here, you doin' okay, Breezy? You've been quieter than a mosquito's fart."

Koa didn't really want to bring up the letter. "Yeah, I don't know, Tug. I guess yesterday just got me thinking. How many times have we come here now?" He reached the top of the ladder and reached down with one foot, grasping at Tug's wrist and hefting him up.

"You got me there," Tug said, rubbing at his whiskers. "Two or three times a week for about five years. Maybe five or six hundred."

"Five or six hundred times. And for what? Is this going to be all there is?" He pointed toward the Crown. "Digging up their trash to try to get through another month?"

"Naw, of course not." Tug gave him a cheerful slap across the shoulders. "Not once we find that pearl."

"Right, the pearl," Koa muttered.

"Sure, the gods love hard-luck cases like ours. You'll see. We'll be rich in no time at all. And if you're worried about that friend of yours, don't be." Tug winked at Koa. "He was near crawlin' out of his britches for you. I could tell."

Koa forced a grin. "Thanks, Tug. I'm sure it'll all work out." He followed his brother into the hedge lizard's shop, feeling like he'd swallowed a sea urchin.

The inside of the shop was dark and smoky, the walls stained black with lantern soot—the hedge lizard preferred the heat and shadow of lantern flame to the cool, bright glowlamps. Koa wrinkled his nose at the reek of burning oil, but Tug, as always, seemed unbothered by it. At first Koa couldn't see the hedge lizard anywhere and scanned the large room for him. The walls were all flowing wood, smooth and rippling, as though the tree had grown itself into the shape of a shop, rather than being carved out. From each of them hung many treasures: watches, rings, golden spectacles, phylacteries, jeweled necklaces, and bracelets. Along one wall were arrayed mystic wonders, all lenses and brass: special cylinders for scrying the distant and the miniscule; automated clocks that whirled without gears; compasses that always pointed toward the moon; key rings that would cry out for you when you lost them. Everything here was touched with the hedge lizard's magic, and they glimmered and twinkled with enchantment.

"I don't think he's here," Koa whispered to Tug, and then two disks that he'd taken for watch faces resolved themselves into the hedge lizard's eyes. He nearly jumped.

"You couldn't get in if I weren't here," the hedge lizard rasped, and he hefted his great bulk toward them, crawling out from behind a ripple in the contours of the shop floor. He was a monitor lizard, the oldest anyone had ever heard of, grown so large and heavy in his age that he seldom stood upright anymore, but leaned on counters and walls, even crawled across the floor on all fours. "What can old Ruduuk do for you today? Did I hear something about a pearl?" His red eyes glittered as he turned his gaze to each of them in turn.

"That's right," Tug said cheerfully. "We've been scroungin' oysters on top of scrap for you. We'll strike it rich one of these days, you watch."

"Good." Ruduuk's forked tongue lapped at the air. "Good. I like you boys. You're like me. You appreciate pretty things." He sank one hand into a jar full of brightly colored stones, lifted up a rattling fistful and watched with a fond expression as they escaped through his fingers like beetles. "What good is a life if you can't fill it with pretty things?"

"Pretty, pfft. Pretty won't buy us a home in the Shoulders, will it? I wouldn't give a flip of the tail for pretty. Him though, he likes pretty just fine, don't you, Koa?"

Koa side-stepped the otter's good-natured jab to his shoulder, but there was no way to dodge the grin. "Yeah, that's me."

"I know you do, little bat. You're like me," the hedge lizard said. "So what'll it be today, boys? What have you brought for me?" He grinned his pointed teeth at them and heaved his huge body across the shop, settling behind his counter: a board of smoothly polished wood, one of the only features in the room carved separately and not hewn from the tree itself.

Tug unstrapped the bag from Koa's wings, unslung his own from his shoulders, and spilled out each onto the hedge lizard's counter. The contents clattered across the polished wood, glittering in the lantern light.

Ruduuk watched with eager eyes as the lost treasures were strewn before his eyes, and even before Tug had finished displaying them all, began snatching up rings or watches to examine them.

When Tug shook out the last of the bags, Ruduuk looked disappointed. "Is this all there is?" he asked, pawing at the empty sacks.

"'Fraid so, Duuky," Tug said. "Can't pull out of the water what the uppity-ups don't throw into it."

Ruduuk scowled at him. "You should speak with more respect, mud-dweller. We were royal once, my family, long ago. So long ago…" He trailed off as though recalling a dream, then straightened. "Not so much this week, then. Next week, more, eh? Bring more. Try fishing around the toes of Saturn. I hear the daughter of the governor there is always dropping her jewelry. Or if you have a mind to try the Crown of Atlas—"

Koa stiffened, but before he could say anything, Tug leaned over the counter and put one stubby finger in Ruduuk's face. "Oy, now you know the Drowned Kingdom is off-limits to scroungers. And you know what happened to his family back there, so how about you not go talking about any grave robbing, eh?"

"Take your finger out of my face, boy," Ruduuk hissed. "Unless you want to test the temperature of my belly."

"That," said Tug, lowering his paw, "is a really terrible threat. You should work on those, Duuky. So. What've we got here? How much?"

The lizard glared at him, but swallowed any further comment. He danced his claws through the many items, sorting them, lifting up to inspect them, and arranging them into little piles. "Thirty rupiah," he decided at last. "Best I can offer. Extra because you boys are my favorite clients."

Koa's wings sagged. "That won't even buy fruit for a week."

"Sorry, little bat. I run a shop, not a charity. I need to eat, too."

Surveying the myriad treasures decorating the shop, Koa doubted whether Ruduuk would ever hunger for anything. The lizard saw him staring around the walls, and cleared his throat. "But if you see something here you want—a nice pair of cufflinks, perhaps—" He broke off, glancing at Koa's rough attire. "Or a new shirt. Hardly been worn. I could give you up to fifty in store credit, if you like. Just a little glamour on it to make you look fresh and dry on rainy days."

Koa stared around the shop, trying to imagine what it would be like to own any of the enchanted items. It wasn't the first time Ruduuk had made the offer, but every time, Koa found he could think of no use for an enchanted cuckoo clock or a turquoise ring, not when their home needed new roofing tiles or a little sister a toy for her birthday. Maybe if he could just find the right thing, some bit of hedge magic that might impress Maiel. He looked at the pocket watches, as always, but they would be far too expensive, and none of them really looked like his father's. His eyes slid over the walls, and then he stopped, curious.

"What are those?" he asked, pointing up to the top of the wall, where three masks hung. They were meant to cover only the eyes, but fashioned in such a way as to exaggerate the wildness of the face, to grant an exotic shape to the eye. It seemed plain they were meant for bats, their bridges narrow so they could perch atop only a slender muzzle. They had been inlaid with jewels or crushed glass and sparkled with entrancing colors. Koa found it difficult to look away.

"Masks for the Firefly Ball," Ruduuk said in a disinterested voice. "Glamoured so that even your own mother won't recognize you while you're wearing them. Used to be in fashion, long ago. Not anymore. Those are antiques." He looked up, and a strange, edged tone came into his voice. "Why, boy? You having thoughts about going upstairs and seeing how the flighted folk live? Are you interested in *going* to a Firefly Ball?"

Koa sifted through hazy memories of the parties he had been to as a pup. Now he thought he recalled seeing other bats wearing those masks. He had faint recollections of being both frightened and enthralled by them.

Tug snorted. "Course he wouldn't. Go up there all hiding, pretending he's someone else just to get a peek at everything they won't let him have? Think we'll just take the money as usual, Ruduuk."

"If I wore one of those," Koa asked softly, "it would disguise me from everyone?" He looked back at Ruduuk.

The lizard's eyes were intent and narrow. "Those? No, those wouldn't do you much good. Everyone would wonder why you were wearing it. Plus it couldn't do much about those scraps of flesh hanging from your arms. Who wouldn't know those?"

"Oh." Koa slumped a little. It was like he'd been looking through a little door into a bright world where everyone was happy and exciting and interesting, and where no one saw his wings, nor knew him as a ladder-knotter. It was a door to a shining place where he didn't have to be Koa, and Ruduuk had slammed it. "I guess we'll take the money after all."

"Now hold on just minute, boy," the lizard said, crawling out from behind the counter. His beady eyes fixed on Koa like they would on a bird he intended to snap up and swallow. "I can see you're interested, and why wouldn't you be? You're like me. You dream of bigger and better things. Always looking up. Yes? If you did want to go to the Firefly Ball, there are ways."

"Ways?" Koa regarded him suspiciously. He had heard Ruduuk talk this way before, usually to customers he was hoping to cheat.

"Well, not for me. Not for that thick-headed brother of yours."

"Hey!" Tug objected, trying to twist his paw out of a cuckoo clock.

"Enchantments prevent all but your kind from visiting the upper world. So I, alas, will never have a chance to see the grand wonder of the Firefly Balls."

"Fireflies ain't even *got* balls," Tug pointed out. He tucked the clock under one arm and tried to wrench his paw free. "Little bastard."

"Let go of the cuckoo," Ruduuk advised in a weary tone.

"But I could go?" Koa asked.

"Not as you are. Those clothes. Those wings. You'd be tossed out in a moment. But with the right enchantment, none would know you." Ruduuk turned and rummaged around behind his counter. There came the sound of clinking glass and thumps. Koa pricked his ears in interest; he had not even known there were shelves back there.

"Here it is." He pushed himself upright and set on the counter a small, cut-glass bottle with a silver cap and a bulb attached. "Eau de Grâce. A powerful enchantment."

"What does it do?" Koa asked in wonder, leaning down to peer at the bottle. Its contents were an opalescent white, shifting and swirling inside the bottle as though continually stirred.

Ruduuk traced his claws down the side of the bottle. "One spray, boy. One spray is all you need to become someone else for a whole night."

"What do you mean, someone else?"

"Someone better. You'll be a fruit bat still, but you'll be noble. Graceful. You'll have poise and elegance. Every movement will be natural. You'll draw the eye. You'll be beautiful. And best of all"—Ruduuk drew a talon along Koa's arm—"no more torn wings. You will be whole again."

Koa pulled his wings closer to his body, shuddering a little at Ruduuk's touch. The scarred flesh felt unpleasant when people touched it. Not painful, just uncomfortable, like a leg that had fallen asleep after being sat upon for too long. "Whole again," he repeated in wonder.

"For a night." Ruduuk shrugged. "Even magic can't undo such harm forever. But sometimes one night is all you need. I know you understand. You're like me. We are not handsome creatures, you and I." He leaned more heavily on the counter, turning over his rough-scaled hands and thumping his long tail against the wall. "Neither of us is very appealing when we move around. What wouldn't either of us give for just one night of easy beauty, eh?"

"Here, now, we don't need to go mucking about with enchantments," Tug said, shoving his way between them. "They come to no good, every time. One night—it's never one night, is it? You get a little taste and then you're trapped."

Koa looked down at the cuckoo clock still stuck around the end of Tug's paw.

"I want to see what the bird looks like," Tug said defensively. "I have to know!"

Koa arched an eyebrow.

"Here, now, that's not the point." Tug waved the clock at him as he might have a finger. "The point is—the point is *magic?* From the *hedge lizard?* You have got to know that's a bad idea."

"There's no need to be rude, boy," Ruduuk said.

"Well, you called me thick-headed first."

"How much?" Koa asked. "How much for one spray?"

A slow smile spread across Ruduuk's face. "Powerful enchantments command high prices. But I'm fond of you. I will let you have a single spray of Eau de Grâce for a thousand rupiah."

Koa stared at him. "Are you joking? A thousand? We could scarcely make that in a year."

"Yeah, how thick do you think we are?" Tug put in. "If what's in that bottle is worth a thousand for every little squirt, how come you're living down here and not in your own palace up in the very tippy-top of Titan?"

Ruduuk flicked his forked tongue. "There wouldn't be time enough in the whole year to administer an economics lesson to you, mud-drinker. Suffice it to say that I know the worth of my enchantments, and your wanting it so terribly neither changes its worth nor justifies your cheating me. If you cannot afford it, then you cannot."

"But it's just sitting there in the bottle, doin' nothing!" Tug protested. "How's that helpin' anyone?" He paused, frowning. "Hang on, what am I arguing with you about this for? This is a bad idea anyway. That was my whole point to begin with. Come on, Koa. Let's go."

Koa's wings sagged. "Yeah, you're right, Tug. Thanks for the offer, I guess," he said to Ruduuk, and turned to go.

The great lizard put a scaled hand on his shoulder. "Hold on just a minute, boy. Do you really want this enchantment so much?"

He let himself dream for a moment. He would be fine and elegant and handsome, ascending the Beards and entering that world of light and music. He would taste the food and drink. He would dance. He would listen to the philosophers speak of the heavens, and watch the sorcerers trace magic through the air. And then, across the great Crown of the Beards, he would spy Maiel, slight, shy, speaking with some of his friends. Their eyes would meet, and Maiel would be instantly drawn to him. They would move toward each other. They would speak little, but embrace, and then dance together, a whirl of easy grace and balance. No strips of flesh would dangle to repulse onlookers. No one would look down on him. No one would shout that he had no right to be there. He would be one of them, accepted, embraced.

One night. One night would be enough. He could be gentle with Maiel, and at the end of the night, tell him the truth about who he was, and then Maiel would know him beyond his disfigurement. From there, who knew what would come next? But without that one night, none of it would happen. He would remain an outcast.

"I really want it," he said, meeting Ruduuk's patient stare.

"Then I will let you have it. One spray. For a favor."

Hope nearly lifted him from his toes. "What favor would be worth that to you?" He was afraid to ask the question, in case it was something unsavory, or worse, illegal. He couldn't afford to get his family in trouble. But just then he felt that he would agree to anything in exchange for that single night.

"Not so special a thing to you. But special to me. All I want you to do is deliver a parcel for me."

Koa looked over his shoulder at Tug, who shrugged. "That sounds easy enough. But why can't you just deliver it yourself?"

"Ah," Ruduuk leaned closer. "Because it must be delivered personally, to the home of an old friend, a flying fox named Toller who lives in the Crown of the Beards, where, if I am not mistaken, your little party is being held tonight. The enchantments around the Crown keep out my kind, your brother's kind, and all who live here in the Lower Kingdoms. All but you, boy. You can move freely past the barriers. That makes you the only one I can ask to deliver this parcel."

"Surely a messenger bat could be summoned," Koa said doubtfully.

"No!" Ruduuk shouted. "I can't trust them. I can't trust any of them." Anger glittered in his red eyes. "There are traitors among them. Many traitors. My old friend Toller seeks equality. He wishes to unite the Upper and Lower Kingdoms, or if not that, at least bring them closer together. It is a cause he has long fought for, and one that has earned him many enemies, including some of those closest to him. They work against him at every turn, all while smiling and pretending to be his friend. I came to him long ago with proof of their enmity, but they had discovered me, and spun lies about me. I never had another chance to speak to him. His enemies make certain that I and all my messages are kept far from him. And I do not know all his enemies. So I cannot put this parcel in the hands of another flying fox. You, dear little Koa, shunned and apart from all of them, are the only one

I can trust. You are the only one who can help me. And that, to me, is worth a thousand rupiah."

Koa looked at the bottle on the counter, its milky contents gleaming a rainbow back at him.

"Don't go for it, little brother," Tug said. "It'll only bring trouble, and you haven't got to go rubbin' strange oils into your hide to get a mate, you know. Well, not *magical* strange oils, anyhow. Plus, how can we know what's in this dodgy parcel? How do we know he's telling the truth?"

Ruduuk glared at Tug. "As for the enchantment, you'll know soon enough that it works. If it doesn't, you won't be delivering my parcel at all, will you?"

"And the parcel?" Koa asked.

The hedge lizard put a hand to his chest. "I swear to you by the Twelve Gods that nothing in there could reasonably harm anyone. It is, as I told you, merely proof of the treachery against Toller. Beyond that, you will have to trust me. Anything worth having requires a risk, doesn't it?

"But the enchantment would only be for one night. What could I do in that time?"

Ruduuk gave Koa a nasty grin filled with pointed teeth. "My boy, you should know better than anyone: one night is all it takes to change everything." He extended a scaly hand. "So. Do we have a deal?"

Koa hesitated, looking at Tug, who shook his head emphatically. He fumbled at his pocket and thumbed over the folded note still concealed there. His heart sped, and before he could stop himself, he took the lizard's fingers in his own, squeezing them with his disfigured wing. "Deal."

"Excellent." Ruduuk's grip grew tighter. He gave a fierce pull, sending Koa stumbling up against the counter, and with his other hand, squeezed the bulb on the perfume bottle. An oily mist diffused into Koa's fur, tiny droplets settling against his membranes.

He pulled back, coughing; the stuff smelled chemical and cloying, almost nauseating. "What'd you do that for?" He rubbed at his muzzle with the back of an arm, trying to lick the unpleasant scent out of his mouth.

Tug pushed up to the counter, his webbed paws clenched into fists. "Yeah, don't think I'm gonna be easy on you just 'cause you're old. And, er, full of magic and stuff." He looked down at the enchanted bottle and backed a step away.

"Oh, surely you didn't think I would let you take the bottle with you?" Ruduuk watched Koa cough and spit with evident amusement. "One spray, that was the deal. Now listen. The enchantment will take hold as soon as moonlight touches it. It will last for about four hours."

"Four hours?" Tug shouted. "That ain't hardly one night. You said the deal was for a night. Moon's up about eight thirty and that gives him only to a little past midnight."

"Which is early morning, surely."

"It's night too!" Tug slammed his fist down on the counter.

Koa put a wing on his shoulder. "It's fine, Tug."

"It *ain't* fine. He's sellin' us mud and tellin' us it's marzipan."

"It's still four hours. Four hours more than I thought I had a chance of."

"That's the spirit, boy," Ruduuk said. "You're like me. Take the deal you've got and make the best you can with it, eh? No use quibbling over an enchantment that can't be altered. Now listen. There are three things you need to remember."

"More surprises, wonderful," grumbled Tug. "If only we'd had some bright and enterprising young otter who'd been loudly saying, 'No, Koa, don't do it, you don't need magic, this guy's dodgier than a found herring,' but sadly there was no one like that in the room, no one to spare you from a ruthless snookering."

"Three things," Ruduuk repeated, glaring at Tug. "First: don't get wet. Rain is fine. Seawater breaks the enchantment."

Koa nodded. That would mean he'd have to take the Canting Bridge to the Ball. The thought dizzied him. The Firefly Ball. He was actually going. It didn't seem real.

"Second: stay away from mirrors. Your reflection will show your true self."

"All right." Koa wondered how many mirrors would be at the Ball. What if he showed up and they were everywhere?

"Finally, and most importantly, you must remember: though you will look and feel whole, you will not be. Those torn wings of yours will not remember skills they never had. You must not attempt to fly."

The thought had not occurred to Koa, but as soon as Ruduuk mentioned it, he longed to attempt it. Surely the knowledge of how to do it was buried deep in his bones and muscles. He was a bat. He was made for flying. If the tears in his wings were repaired, what could be the harm in just giving them a few test flaps? Even if he couldn't go anywhere, he longed to know what it was like.

Ruduuk must have seen a dreamy look in Koa's eyes, because he growled low. "Promise me, boy. Your favor is no good to me if you get hurt."

"All right, all right. No flying."

"And?"

"Don't touch sea water, and stay away from mirrors. I've got it."

Ruduuk regarded him, his brow ridge lowered. "All right. Wait right here." He ducked down behind the counter again, so low that Koa couldn't see him. His long, scaled tail waved in the air for a minute, and more rummaging sounds came from below. He muttered something low and sibilant that Koa couldn't make out, and then there was the sound of paper crinkling.

"Here we are." Ruduuk stood and placed a small parcel on the counter. It was small and flat, about the size of a thin book, wrapped in brown paper and tied with twine. "Now listen closely. You must deliver this message to the house of Toller the Magician. Not on the front door, not even to his hand at the party, but to his house. I cannot risk his enemies seeing it. Only in his house can we be certain that he will be able to read it safely. Do you understand?"

Koa nodded. "But what if I can't get in?"

Ruduuk bared his teeth. "You will find a way. If you do not, then you will have failed to uphold our bargain, and I will hold you as a debtor, accountable for every rupiah up to the thousandth you owe."

Chapter 6

D o you see anything yet?" Koa checked his wings, but they were still the same scarred tatters as always. He wondered if he felt something. There might be a tingling; he wasn't sure. The nauseating odor of the unguent still clung to his fur, pervading the mustier aroma of their hideout.

"No, nothing yet. And no moon neither. It ain't comin' up faster just 'cause you want to look pretty," Tug said, staring at the sky, which had been dark for some time now. He had been grouchy ever since leaving Ruduuk's shop.

"I still think we should have gone over there first."

"That'd be a sight, if we couldn't find some place for you to hide at moonrise, getting' all magicked in front of people."

"But it's going to look weird when I cross the bridge. People are going to wonder why I didn't fly."

Tug scowled and tossed an oyster shell across the floor. "Should have thought of that before you got enchantified."

"What's with you, anyway? I'm excited about this. Why can't you be?"

His brother grimaced. "Because, Koa, you made a deal with the hedge lizard."

"So? It's not like he's ever done anything bad, right? I mean he's a bit of a cheat, but so what?"

"So what, until he cheats *you*," Tug pointed out, then sighed. "I dunno. He just gives me the jeebs. Like what's up with him stuffed away in that creepy old shop? Why ain't he got any friends hanging around, or family? What's up with him giving you dodgy parcels to lose in rich folk's houses? That's not normal, you know. And all that talk about politics and enemies. You believe a word of it?"

Koa flushed, feeling angry and unsure why. "Look, I don't know, Tug. I'm not part of that world, am I? That's all I'm trying to do, is get back to it, just a little bit. If I can remember what it was like, what my parents were like, then maybe I can figure out who I am, too."

"Who you are?" Tug looked back at Koa with an expression of disbelief. "You get a crack on the head? You're my know-it-all little brother who plays a rope like a fiddle and mopes at dinner and wouldn't know the taste of a good fish if it gave him remedial courses at Seafood Academy on good fishiness and then leapt down his throat screaming 'I'm delicious!' What more do you need to know? You think some frou-frou bats with sticks up their bums are gonna know something about you that you don't?"

"Maybe. I can't know until I try. It's where I would have been raised, you know, if the Great Storm hadn't come." Koa paused. "Besides, wouldn't *you* like a chance to live up there, in that world, with all the stuff they've got?"

"What, up in the Crowns? All waving back and forth in the wind and the world all swirly down below? Sounds wretched. I'd be pissin' myself night and day and you lot down here would be holdin' out your paws sayin', 'I sure wish this awful-smelling rain would let up.'"

"Yeah, but not if you'd been raised up there. You'd be used to it. Given the choice, wouldn't you rather have been raised surrounded by all that wealth and magic?"

"What?" Tug snorted. "Not a chance. I'm an otter; I don't need to be prancing about at the ends of thin little twigs instead of down in the water. Come on, Breezy, you know me better than that. Down here's family, down here's my people, and I—oh." He muttered a choice swear.

"Yeah, see? You'd have to know, right? And besides, there's Maiel. If I can just get another chance to see him, to get to talk to him without anyone else staring or poking fun—"

Tug leered at him. "Aye, there's the rub, isn't it? And by rub, I mean that you're hoping you'll get to—"

"I know what you mean, mudbrain."

"You better watch that filthy mouth of yours up there," Tug said, shaking a stubby finger at him. "Or else they're all gonna know that you're—"

"Quiet," Koa interrupted him. The silvery lip of the moon glimmered on the edge of the eastern sea.

"What? I was only joking, you know that."

"No, I mean… I feel something." He stood on his toes, trying to stretch upward into the moonlight. The tips of his ears and the top of his head felt cool and tingly, like they'd been dipped into soda water.

Tug began working up a skeptical expression, but then his mouth hung open. "You're right, it's all comin' down from your ears, like someone's washin' the ugly off of you from top to bottom."

The cool sensation spread downward, and Koa lifted his fingers to his face. Beneath them, his coarse, matted fur turned fine and silky. He felt his muzzle grow more slender and elegant, and then the sensation moved to his wings. Wondering, he raised them into the moonlight. His gnarled and misshapen limbs shimmered and straightened, the long rags of his flesh melting

71

together. Expensive-looking clothes wrapped themselves around his body, his rough shirt softening into a silver vest that glinted with metallic blue, open at the front to frame his lean chest and belly, his fur now immaculately groomed and cleaned, short and soft. Matching trousers encircled his legs, with vents to admit his wings and tail. He could not discern how they stayed on him, but they looked similar to the clothes he had seen other bats wearing, which clung appealingly whether hanging from one's feet or walking about on them. The cool feeling washed down over his toes, which were now encircled with silver and blue bands. He stretched his wings wide open, and they were full and taut, the membranes translucent, seeming almost to emanate a warm, amber light, and inlaid or tattooed with a sparkling gold filigree that concealed the arteries within.

He had wings, *real wings*. "How do I look?" he asked Tug, turning slowly. He kept his wings wide open, feeling them catch the air as wings were supposed to.

"Not like yourself," Tug answered, shaking his head in plain wonder.

"Good." He wished he had a mirror so that he could see himself, but then, he reminded himself, a mirror would do no good. "What time is it?"

"Er." Tug rummaged around until he found their old brass telescope, went to the door, and peered out at the great clock that hung near the top of the Great Drinker. He kept looking back at Koa, staring in such amazement that it took him three times before he managed to successfully report the time. "Eight forty-two. Best to start splashin' back when you hear midnight, eh?"

Koa nodded. "Okay."

Tug gripped his shoulders in both paws, then grimaced. "You're all twiggy and soft now. Don't feel right. Listen. I know you got to do this now, but if something goes wrong, don't take it hard, okay? You got all of us down here behind you."

"Thanks, Tug. I'll be fine. Don't worry."

He turned to go, and Tug shouted, "Hang on, Breezy, ain't you weighin' a little less than you should?"

"What?"

Tug held out Ruduuk's parcel. "Woulda been a bit awkward, gettin' there and havin' to come all the way back. Here. Put it in your cloak."

"I have a cloak?" Koa craned his neck to look over his shoulder and saw long folds of black fabric draped down his back. It was so light that he could barely sense it, but now that he was aware of it, he could feel its tickle against his wings.

Tug tucked the parcel into a pocket of Koa's cloak. "This is all going to go so mudding well. I can already tell."

Chapter 7

There was no one to watch Koa's progress across the Canting Bridge, for which he was grateful. Traversing it with undamaged wings was an entirely different experience. If he stretched his arms open even a little, the wind would catch his sails and pull intensely at them, threatening to tear him away from the swaying bridge. It was at once frightening and exhilarating. The wind yearned to lift him up and carry him away, and he yearned to ride it. But he knew that Ruduuk was right: he had no experience flying; nor had he built up the proper muscles. Within moments, he would tire or lose his orientation and then crash into the sea. So he kept his arms close to his sides, sidling step by step across the bridge, a journey that seemed to take forever, wasting precious time he could not afford.

When he reached the Bearded Kingdom, he could already hear the music of the Firefly Ball, strings and flutes and brass echoing the strains of some jaunty dance above. He climbed the winding paths up the tree, passing few people on the way, and most of those carried lanterns and peered into the darkness, never giving him a second glance. With the nearly full moon rising in the eastern sky and his natural night vision, he found it easy to see, but every time a lantern went by, its streaky image throbbed in his vision for several minutes, and when he lifted a wing to rub at his eyes, the wind would catch it and threaten to spin him off his balance.

He climbed higher, and the music grew louder, the lights of the party brighter. Past the Shoulders, he heard the chatter and laughter of the other bats above, and there, just below the Head, the path ended. The Nets were strung out above him—a broad and expansive lattice of thick rope and thin mesh. Meant to catch anything that fell from the world above, the Nets protected the Head and Crown from loss, and the Lower Kingdoms from having dropped articles rain down on their heads all the time. They didn't always work, of course. Heavy or sharp objects often tore through the Nets, smaller ones slipped through the mesh, or holes and rents, and the shiniest were often carried off by gulls or jackdaws before they could be recovered by netcombers. The ocean was filled with fallen treasures that the Nets had failed to capture.

Strictly speaking, no one but official netcombers was allowed onto the Nets, but from time to time, people used branches and installed ladders that led to the upper Kingdoms. These were the only way up without flying. Koa found a rope ladder and climbed it upside down, feeling more comfortable getting a solid grip on each rung with his flexible toes, and he noticed that his clothes didn't slide up his body or dangle around his ears when he hung. He supposed they must be enchanted, as he didn't feel them gripping or clinging in any way. Idly he wondered, if you doused a bat with seawater, would all his clothes just fall off of him? He giggled and then thought of Maiel and felt a different kind of lightheaded.

The climb up into the Head of the Bearded Kingdom was a long and rather arduous one, and Koa didn't know the way. Several times, he found himself ascending a ladder to a branch that went nowhere, and he had to turn around and head back down. He glanced at the moon and wondered with a sinking heart how much time he had wasted already. But the next ladder climbed high, taking him above the broad brown valleys of the Nets and through the edge of the enchantment that protected the Upper Kingdoms. He felt the magic as he passed through it, the lightest of touches, like a breath against his skin and fur. Anyone other than a bat would have found it impossible to continue. "Like climbing into a bubble made of sticky molasses," his brother Demel had said—he'd been curious about the enchantment and tested it long ago. "The farther you go, the stickier and thicker the molasses get, until you just can't climb another inch."

But now Koa was beyond it. He had climbed higher than anyone in his whole family had ever been. Except for his birth parents, of course. And uncles and aunts and grandparents that he'd never known, all lost in the Great Storm. It was they who would have taken him in after his parents died. He wasn't the first young bat to have torn wings, but others, as far as he knew, had had relatives to adopt them. All his were gone. After the storm, his otter parents had asked around, trying to find someone who recognized the foundling pup, someone who could take care of him, but many other lives had been lost that night. There were deaths to mourn, there was rebuilding to be done, and no one had time to look after a single injured orphan.

"Heartless, they were," his mother had commented once. "Heartless not to care. How could they take one look at you and not love you? I wouldn't have given you over to a single one of them even if they'd changed their minds." And she'd never taken Koa back to see the bats again, except to a doctor once or twice. His father still asked around from time to time, but if Koa had any other relatives, they remained silent, so he had remained in the world below.

Until tonight. Now he was beyond the enchantment, and the moonlight shone bright silver, and the light of the party above matched it in gold. He climbed toward the music. The ladder did not end at the top of a branch, but at the bottom of one. This puzzled him for a moment—how was he supposed to climb off? But then he saw the carefully woven thatch of branches leading away from the ladder above, and he realized that they were footholds. The world of the flying foxes was upside down, at least in part. He reached up with one foot and gripped the branches with his toes, wings spreading as though he could catch himself if he fell. He swayed out over emptiness.

He was not unused to being upside down; his bedroom had poles across the ceiling so that he could hang from them while he slept, and he frequently swung ears-down while repairing ropes and ladders. It was more comfortable; his body felt right somehow, and his thoughts flowed more freely and easily. But when moving about, he had always stood upright or crawled on foot and wing. He had not remembered the world of his childhood being upside down, and it was strange to him that he would have forgotten such a thing.

Unaccustomed to the swinging walk that would move him beneath the branches of the trees, he feared that his gait would be obviously clumsy and awkward, but he found that his movements felt natural, and even easy. Another effect of the Eau de Grâce, he supposed, granting him the agility and poise that suited his disguise. It took a moment for his perspective to adjust—up became down, low became high—and then he followed the path of interlaced branches, which must have been carefully woven as they grew over decades, even centuries, to form the road down into the Head of the Bearded Kingdom.

Beauty and wealth met his eyes. The branches of the great tree twined everywhere, shaped by magicians into pathways and winding pillars lined with flowers and heavy fruit. Glowlamps dangled upward from the floor on long, swaying vines that could be reeled down to illuminate something close by in light of any color. Ladders and woven staircases linked floor and ceiling to dizzying effect, with flying foxes strolling about hanging from their feet, or standing on the ceiling above with equal ease. Koa's head whirled; it was difficult to remember which direction was which. He plucked a leaf from a nearby branch and let it go, watching it twirl and dive to the ceiling above, where others of his kind played and talked. He could understand why so many objects were lost, dropped into the Nets above.

Few homes here were carved into the bark of the tree or nestled in between crooks of branches and folds in the heart-wood. They were fashioned, grown carefully with time and magic from the branches themselves, decorated with flowers of various shapes and colors that grew from the walls of the houses. Everywhere was beauty and light and life.

It wasn't what he had expected. He had thought his memories of his childhood world true, but he saw now that what he recalled was no more than a memory of a dream of a memory. The old home in his mind, wide and empty and dark, bore little resemblance to this place, and yet it was achingly familiar, calling to him in the manner of an old song, the sort that itches just at the edge of one's recollection, yet whose melody remains elusive; or like the forgotten face of an old friend whose name one still remembers.

He stepped down into the world of moonlight and glow-lamps and stared, his mission forgotten. Someone touched the edge of his wing, and he nearly snatched it away self-consciously before remembering himself. "Sir? Are you all right?"

He turned, and saw a female bat standing next to him, her eyes full of unguarded concern. No one had ever called him sir before.

"Er, yes, I'm fine. Thank you."

"You looked a bit lost."

"Oh, I…" he fumbled for words. "Did you ever step out of a room and forget where you were going?"

"All the time!" She smiled. "Perhaps you were on your way to the Ball?"

"Yes," he said, relieved. "Of course. Is that where you're headed?"

"I was thinking about it." She looked him up and down. "Sure. Why not?" She stepped closer to his side.

Uncomfortably, he realized she expected him to lead, and he wasn't quite certain where to go. He twitched his ears, finding the source of the music, and decided on a broad path that descended down through the Head and into the top of the Crown. When he focused on it, he could hear the sounds of loud talk and the clinking of glasses, so that was almost certainly the place. He set off in that direction, and as soon as he started, the female bat at his side seemed to forget her concern. She chattered about who was likely to be there tonight and who hadn't come last time, and hadn't the music been dreadful, but the decorating was far superior, and there were rumors that the Balls would be put on hold for a month—a whole month!—due to low supplies and the drought that afflicted the East, but some said that the rainy season would be especially heavy this year, and that meant little flying and lots of stockpiling and staple fruits rather than delicacies unless they could get some of the larger boating clans to make more frequent shipments.

Koa listened to all of this with bewildered attentiveness, trying to make approving or surprised noises in the correct places, but he had little understanding of anything she was talking about. And he found the sparkling world of the upper Kingdoms so fascinating that he could scarcely pay attention. He followed the broad path through the branches, his toes instinctively gripping with each step, until it made a winding spiral down into the Crown, and here the music grew louder. Colored lights spun and flickered below, and as they descended, one whizzed up to them, a fist-sized globe of brilliant violet light that hovered, buzzing for a moment before Koa's nose before zipping away again. He smiled to cover his astonishment, trying to blink the glare of it out of his eyes.

His companion rolled her eyes and said something about how the fireflies had grown more brazen lately and wasn't it just a little annoying at times? And then they continued down and into the world of the Firefly Ball.

Koa could not remember seeing so many flying foxes together in all his life. They clustered along the floor and ceiling of the Crown, settling together with drinks, dancing, and sometimes flapping back and forth. The room was filled with fireflies, floating spheres of bright lights in every color, pulsing with the music, zipping and whirling around. His companion spread her wings wide, and several pink fireflies clustered within them, shining their lights brighter and illuminating her membranes a brilliant carnation.

Koa stared around in awe. In time with the music, flying foxes all through the ball spread their wings as part of the dance, and the fireflies lit their wings, the ball pulsing with their multicolored radiance. He stretched out his own, and immediately several green fireflies clustered behind him, making his membranes glow a viridian light like the sun behind leaves.

He laughed in delight, and his companion giggled. "You act like you've never even seen a Firefly Ball before."

"It's been a long time," he confessed.

"Well then, come on!" She took his wing in hers and pulled him down into the tumult of music and light and dance.

He followed, his feet finding the tempo of the music and moving with it of their own accord. He had never danced; his balance had always been unsteady, and quick movements made his rent sails flap and dangle in unappealing ways. Better to keep his wings at his sides and move carefully. But now, here, his wings were untorn, so he unfolded them, and found himself bobbing and swaying to the music as though it flowed through him and propelled him. He didn't know whether it was the music or the magic that gave him grace. He knew only that he felt it, and that when it moved him, everything else that he was became unimportant. He was carried on the music as he might have been on air.

The female bat swayed lithely at his side. "You dance pretty well for someone who never goes to balls. What made you come tonight?"

"I'm looking for someone." He had to raise his voice to be heard over the music.

"Someone special?" she asked, looking disappointed.

"Yeah." He stared out over the crowd, and the realization of his mistake slowed his feet. There must be hundreds of people here. How would he ever find one flying fox in the middle of this huge, chaotic crowd? He turned back to ask if she knew a bat named Maiel, and where he might be, but she was gone, disappeared into the crowd.

He pulled his wings in tight, worried. Supposing he couldn't find Maiel at all? The whole enchantment would be for nothing. It would have been far easier to find him some other night, *any* night other than the Firefly Ball.

Well, he decided, he'd never find him there, in the middle of the dance, so he made his way through the crowd to one of the more open areas. Here, long silver tables hung from the ceiling by thin cords of a weave Koa didn't recognize. They were laden with piles of strange fruits and foods, few of which he could identify, but most of which looked appetizing. The smell rising from them was mouthwatering, and Koa's stomach rumbled as he recalled he hadn't eaten his dinner the night before.

Imitating the other bats, he walked above one of the hanging tables and reached down to take a dish with an assortment of fruit: thin, circular slices of an orange thing that smelled of honey, piled with dark things that he thought were berries, but on closer inspection appeared to be some sort of jelly drizzled with a foamy cream. It broke into spice and sweetness and juice in his mouth, a flavor of such surprising delicacy and richness that he almost dropped the plate—and looked up to see fine nets strung above the dining area, presumably meant to catch the dinnerware of those who had done just that. Never in his life had he tasted anything so delicious. He gulped it down, heedless of any stares. He took another dish, this one a bowl filled with little blue globes that were astonishingly cold, but dissolved on his tongue into floral airiness.

"Good, aren't they?" an older female bat said, noting his enjoyment. "Just started getting those this year. Filo has them flown in from Terai. I can't get enough of them."

Koa let another dissipate into flavors of jasmine and honey on the roof of his mouth. "Amazing," he agreed. He handed his dish to a passing waiter with a tray. "I'm sorry, but do you know any way to find a person here? I'm supposed to meet someone, but I'll never manage it in this crowd."

The older bat eyed him, tipping a glass toward her muzzle and drinking deeply from it. "Whoever she is, she shouldn't have let *you* off the wing. Your dance card must have a waiting list."

"Dance card?" he stammered, flustered. What did he look like?

She shook her head. "Just an old, forgotten tradition. Have you asked the coat check?" She pointed a wing toward the spiral branch by which Koa had entered the ball. From this angle, he could see that nestled beneath the ramp was a lit nook with a bat standing inside. As she stretched out her wing, several pale blue fireflies lit it from behind. She swatted at them with both wings. "Go away, you bothersome creatures." Looking embarrassed, she turned back to Koa. "They grow tiresome after a while, don't they?"

He stretched his wings wide, and they lit green again. He wondered if the same fireflies had been following him all evening. "I don't know, I rather like them."

"Well. You're young yet, aren't you? Anyway, ask the coat checks. They keep an eye on everyone who comes in. Have to, you know, in case someone important shows up."

"Thank you, madam," he said, dipping his head.

She shrieked with laughter. "Madam! Well, aren't you sweet. If you can't find your friend, you pretty young thing, come back and see me, won't you?"

"Of course," he answered, flustered, and then hurried back through the crowd before she could see his ears darken.

When Koa approached the coat check beneath the ramp, the elderly bat manning it gave Koa a searching look. He hung from his perch with his back straight, keeping his wings at his sides, and when he moved, did so with slow and deliberate movements. His station was woven of vines and thin branches and was filled with cloaks and umbrellas and various bags and purses. "May I take your cloak, sir?"

"Of course." Koa only now realized how very warm he was and untied the clasp around his shoulders, handing the cloak to the other bat. The breeze against his wings felt delightful. "I'm sorry, but I wonder if you've seen a friend of mine enter. He's about my age" —he realized abruptly he had no idea what age he appeared to be, and fervently hoped it was true—"and his name is Maiel."

The bat's eyes widened slightly at the name. "A friend of yours, you say? He's here, of course. Arrived moments earlier. If you are looking for him, I believe he was headed for the pools."

"Pools?"

The bat gestured up toward the floor of the Crown, where, across the hollow, Koa could see shimmering circles of water with bats reclining in them.

"Oh, of course. Thank you." He frowned, staring up at the floor, dozens of feet above his head. "How do I—" He started to ask how to reach it, then bit his tongue as he realized the obvious answer: fly. Well, he'd just have to find another way up.

He thanked the bat and headed off, looking for a way to reach the floor. The spiral ramp was an obvious solution, but its path wrapped around the floor and into the ceiling of the Head. He decided to climb it anyway, and found that near the floor of the Crown, a little side path twined away from the main ramp. He followed this, hanging from his toes, and discovered that it ended in a round loop, the floor about six feet above his head, and here he could curl up, hold onto the path with his fingers, let go with his toes, and drop down to his feet.

He felt a moment of dizzying disorientation as up and down reversed in his mind again, and he got used to his weight pulling him down instead of stretching him out. Then he followed the broad limb of the tree back into the hollow of the Crown.

People stared at him as he passed, making him feel self-conscious, but he was unable to keep from gazing back. Here, where they did not have to cling to vines and branches, the bats moved more freely. Some danced, and others played a kind of game with the fireflies, flashing their wings brightly and sending the fireflies bouncing from person to person. Koa watched with some interest, but was unable to sort out the rules. Other bats reclined on large pillows, some with surprising intimacy, nuzzling at muzzles or enfolding each other in their wings.

Beyond these, Koa found the pools: wide basins of clear water set into hollows in the branch. Flying foxes reclined or splashed in them, most fully clothed, some less so. The fireflies had no fear of the water. They dived beneath the surface as though it were only air, zig-zagging under the water, leaving streaks of light and illuminating a belly here, a thigh there, then erupting from the surface with a spray of droplets. As their lights were not extinguished, Koa supposed the water must be fresh, and not seawater. He moved alongside the pools, scanning the faces of their inhabitants, and trying not to notice the way they stared back. He recognized none of them. He was just about to turn away in dismay, when one of the smaller bats near the end turned his way. Round glasses glinted in the golden light of a firefly's glow.

He hurried over to the edge of the pool. "Maiel?"

The other bat's glasses were fogged white with steam from the pool. He lifted them from his muzzle and blinked up at Koa. "I'm sorry, do I know you?"

"Er—" He cursed himself for not thinking of that. "N—no, perhaps not." Charming. He was supposed to be charming. "But... but well I know of you, Master Maiel!" He gave a low bow. "Truly, your beauty is justifiably renowned."

Maiel stared up at him with unfocused eyes, then screwed up his face. "My *beauty* is *renowned?* Renowned where? I'm in university for law. Are you trying to mock me or something?"

"No! No!" Koa stammered. He searched his memory for scenes from his books, and realized with a panic that every line from them might seem foolish to a modern, young bat. "All I'm trying to say is that, uh, is that your—your dance card must have quite a waiting list. You know?"

Maiel covered a giggle with a wing. "My what? Listen, sir, I don't know who you think you were looking for, but you *really* didn't find him. You better keep looking." With that, he turned and settled back into the pool once more.

"No, wait," Koa cried. "Please wait." He stumbled into the pool, praying that it wasn't actually seawater. Rather, he meant to stumble, but it turned into sort of a graceful hop, the water barely splashing. It was surprisingly hot, almost uncomfortably so, and he could feel it soaking into his trousers and making them want to sag downward. Maiel looked back at him in surprise.

"I'm sorry. I don't mean to sound strange. It's just that I've come such a long way to see you and I'm—I guess I'm not very good at trying to talk to people I like."

"You came a long way? You're not from here?"

"Well, not exactly." Koa looked down as a pale blue firefly swirled curiously around his submerged toes. A half-truth was better. Easier to remember. "My name is, er"—he scrambled for something appropriate—"Kawa. I've been away a long time. And then I saw you in the Lower Kingdoms the other day, and I had to come and find you. Please, couldn't we just talk for a bit?"

Maiel frowned. "You said you saw me down below?"

"Yes, si—Yes, I've just returned from a long trip to the east, and I had deliveries for some of the shops below."

The flying fox sucked at his teeth. "Hm. Well, perhaps we could talk for a moment or two." He stood, stepping up out of the pool, and the water disappeared from his clothing, leaving it dry and light as though it had never been submerged. Rivulets ran from the points of his wings and pooled around his toes. "Let's go someplace a little quieter, hm?"

"That sounds nice." Koa followed him, grateful to be out of the water, as the heat had begun to make him pant.

"Mind if we walk? My wings are wet."

"No no, that's fine," Koa said, relieved at the excuse. "To tell the truth, I'm rather tired anyway."

Maiel wiped his glasses dry on his white shirt and settled them back on his muzzle. When he looked at Koa again, his eyes widened. "Oh! I, er—" His ears darkened.

"Is something wrong?"

The smaller bat stared at him. "No, I—I just didn't expect that you would be so—never mind." He stared a little longer. "We should go," he said finally, brushing his fingers at Koa's wing.

At his touch, the fur lifted down Koa's spine, and all the fireflies seemed to glow more brightly.

He followed Maiel away from the pools, down a long Arm of the Beards, away from the party. The noise and lights receded into the distance, though he noticed the fireflies followed, his own cluster of deep green and Maiel's of pale blue hovering overhead.

They traveled down the Arm and then over the side, hanging upside down and moving along footholds carved or shaped into the bark. The world swung below, dark and peaceful. Eventually Maiel stopped, stepping out of the path a little, looking down the length of the tree. Koa couldn't help smiling at him—he was so perfect, his ears perked, dark eyes glittering behind his lenses as he gazed out at the night, velvety wings wrapped about him, glistening with the damp of the pools.

"Look at them. The Lower Kingdoms," Maiel said. There was a softness in his voice that Koa could not interpret. "Already most of them are asleep. You know why?"

Koa stared down at the world below. Reflections of the party lights glittered in the water, as though the top of the tree had sunk beneath the surface and still shone up at him. Above them, the trunk of the Bearded Kingdom rose high, little warm spots of light tracing its paths. Glowlamps shone in the windows of homes and shops here and there, but many more were dark. "Because they can't see in the dark, I suppose."

"Because they have to *labor*," Maiel said. "While we're up here partying, they get whatever rest they can. They'll be up before the sun is, leaving their families and the meager comforts of their beds to go and slave away in the heat just to make sure they and their children have enough to eat for the day."

"It isn't that bad," Koa objected.

"Well, that's what we tell ourselves, isn't it? They're used to that life. They like it. They're suited for it. That's what we all say. But it's just to make us feel better. You must know that. You've been outside the Kingdoms, and you deal with the lower classes. You've seen what it's like."

Koa fidgeted. "Well, yes, but I don't think they're unhappy, mostly. I suppose it would be nice if they *could* come up here, now and then." He tried to imagine a whole horde of otter pups rampaging through the Firefly Ball, or worse, some of Tug's old friends given free run. "Although it's possible they'd just wreck everything."

Maiel frowned, his back going stiff. "Just because people are poor, that doesn't make them criminals, you know."

"That's not what I'm saying." The conversation was getting confusing. "I'm just saying that maybe not everyone would appreciate all this."

"Oh, I know what you're saying. I've heard it a hundred times before, and I'm sick of it. If we let them in, we're just asking for another storm."

"Look, when flying foxes come down to the lower levels, it's no better. They're always getting in the way, interfering with work, causing scenes. They've got no idea how to behave when they—" He paused. "What do you mean, asking for another storm?"

Maiel shrugged. "You know, because they caused the Great Storm. That's why we put the barrier up in the first place."

Koa nearly lost his grip on the tree. "The lower classes caused the Great Storm?" He struggled to keep the shock from his voice.

Maiel stared at him. "I mean, nobody can prove it, but everyone knows *someone* did. That's what they say, anyway. You *have* been away, haven't you? Have you really never heard that?"

Koa shook his head, his thoughts whirling. How could someone cause a storm? "How do they know?"

"Well, it wasn't a natural storm. No ordinary wind could fell one of the Kingdoms, of course. Besides, it died as soon as Atlas fell. So it must have been sorcery. And since everyone says no bat would ever dare summon a storm, it must have been someone from the Lower Kingdoms. So now there are all sorts of protections in place. Like the barrier."

The lights of the Kingdoms twinkled below. Koa watched them, wondering if someone down there could have done such a terrible thing, and why. It was unthinkable. Everyone depended on the Kingdoms, not just the bats. "I don't think they could have done it. It's our—it's *their* home just as much as it is ours. I can't think of any reason why someone down there would do that. They're good people."

He was quiet after that, and when Maiel didn't say anything, he looked over to see the smaller bat blinking at him with admiration. "I've never met any other bat who thought that way. This is what I've been saying! To treat them with fear and suspicion, to exclude them as we've been doing, just because of one terrible thing that happened long ago—this is wrong." He smacked the fingers of one wing into the palm of the other, swaying a little as the breeze caught him. "All we do is push them further away, make enemies of them when we should be allies. We ought to be bringing them in, welcoming them, accepting them. I know not many others dare say it, but I think the barrier should go. Don't you agree?" Maiel smiled up at Koa, his brown eyes wide and hopeful.

Koa felt himself melting. "Of course I do," he said. He wasn't sure if he'd agreed before, but he did now. He thought if Maiel said the moon was triangular and spun in circles, he'd agree.

Maiel beamed back at him. "Do you want to go and have a drink? Maybe a dance?"

Koa dared to put his fingers on Maiel's soft wing. "There's nothing in the whole world I'd like more."

In a happy daze, he followed Maiel back along the Arm and into the music and light of the Firefly Ball. They worked across the floor, weaving around other flying foxes who danced and bobbed and swung each other in time with the music, and climbed their way to the ceiling along the spiral path. Koa knew without the enchantment, he'd have tripped and stumbled or lost his grip a dozen times—switching from standing on his feet to hanging from them wasn't easy, and required a trick of balance he'd never had the opportunity to master. But the magic made him as graceful and natural as a native.

The fireflies had changed their tricks, no longer pulsing behind opening wings, but forming loops and spirals around the dancers, surrounding them in luminescent arcs of brilliant colors. Koa's own green fireflies outlined his wings continually, making him look like a living drawing, while Maiel's pale blue ones formed a fanciful and ever-shifting series of hats atop his head.

At the other side of the ceiling, they reached the gleaming silver tables that hung from the ceiling. Maiel selected one that held a series of crystal glasses and led Koa to it. He reached up, took one, and handed it to Koa. It held a clear liquid filled with tiny bubbles that clung to the edge of the glass, rising to the edge and bursting on the surface. Koa blinked at it in fascination, and gave it a sniff. The scent of fruit and something more acrid and unpleasant stung at his nostrils, and he wrinkled his nose. Surely no one could care for such a foul drink. But he wasn't about to look uncultured in front of Maiel. He looked back for the bat, who was staring up at the table full of glasses, his brow furrowed.

"Everything okay?" he asked.

Maiel blinked at him. "Oh! Yes. I was just trying to remember when I'd had this vintage before." He reached up and took a glass, smiling at Koa. "I really think you'll like it."

Mimicking Maiel's movements, Koa tipped the glass down toward his muzzle, the liquid flowing over the roof of his mouth. He dipped his tongue into it, and the bubbles tickled at it. The flavor was strange, not at all like the stinging scent, but complex: sweet, tangy, and bitter all at once. However enjoyable the taste, the liquid burned at his throat when he swallowed. He was sure if not for the enchantment, he would have choked and coughed.

"You see?" Maiel said.

"Remarkable," Koa managed, and took another draught from his glass. The stuff was already warming his stomach. He wondered if it were magical in some way.

Maiel tapped his glass with the clink of one claw. "Finish up and we'll take another before our dance. No reason we shouldn't enjoy it, hm?"

"No reason," Koa agreed, and he drained his glass. The libation's flavor seemed to improve with each sip, and the burning in his throat had suffused into a warm, pleasant glow.

Maiel let go his glass, and it dropped toward the floor above, but it didn't fall far before a little swarm of pink fireflies clustered inside it, carrying it away. Koa laughed and imitated him, his own glass captured by a group of white fireflies. "Do you suppose they mind?" he asked, watching the glowing creatures float off with his glass.

"They're not real," Maiel said, chuckling. "Just conjurations. But you know that, of course."

"Of course."

They each took another glass and headed off toward the large group of dancing bats. Maiel took Koa's wing in his fingers as they walked, and he had to fight to keep from shivering at the touch. No one ever touched his wings but him. Koa's fingers and membranes brushing against his own was somehow achingly intimate, and he found himself nudging back, nestling closer.

Before joining the dance, they both drained their glasses and let them go, and then Maiel pulled Koa into the whirl. He moved in time with the music so naturally, it was as though the notes caught at something in his limbs and chest and pulled him along. His toes clasped the fine mesh of the woven branches of the ceiling inerrantly, and as the bats moved with the music, so the whole canopy dipped and swayed.

A general light-headedness overtook Koa as he moved with Maiel, and for a moment, he worried that the drinks might indeed have been enchanted, but in the next he decided that he didn't care. He was happy, happier than he had ever been. This was his world. This was where he belonged, here, lit by the colors and moving with the music as though he were part of it. He held Maiel's wing in his own and they both spread them wide, and then he spun the smaller bat close.

The music slowed, and so did their steps and style. Koa folded his wings about Maiel, and Maiel put his head to Koa's chest, and they swayed gently to the sound of reeds and strings. The whole world rocked below them. Koa dipped his head and breathed in, smelling Maiel's light musk and the traces of a floral cologne with spicy hints. He squeezed at the smaller bat, and Maiel nestled closer, breathing a happy sigh into his chest fur and looking up at him. The reflections of a thousand colored lights sparkled in his eyes.

This moment, Koa thought. It's perfect. I could spend the rest of my life here.

Maiel patted at his chest. "Let's go."

"Go?" Koa asked in dismay.

"To the top of the Crown. There won't many people up there now. We can find a quiet spot."

Excitement surged through him. "Okay."

He followed Maiel through the crowd again, and this time they took a path off to the side, past a group of bats who seemed to be asleep and hung with their wings folded about them, past a row of branch-woven enclosures whose occupants held out shimmering fabrics or sparkling pendants and called for the partygoers to come and try them on. They climbed another loop and switched from hanging to standing, and from there ascended up into the very top of the Crown.

It was quieter here, though the sound of the music still filtered through the branches below. Koa took a deep breath and looked around. Stars glittered overhead. The moon cast a pale glow across the broad field of branches. They were thinner here, and leaves and branch were knitted together into living paths that wound across the treetop. Here and there, errant limbs rose higher, jutting up like leafy spires. The warm lights of homes glowed from within their warps—though from what Koa could see, these were more palace than home, towering in size, with dozens of windows. They bloomed with multicolored flowers, and vines laden with fruit hung from their roofs, dangling orange and yellow orbs whose sweetness Koa could smell even from a distance. One of these must have been where the royal family of the Beards had lived, back when were still kings and queens.

Maiel sighed. "Beautiful at night, isn't it?"

Koa suddenly remembered to close his mouth. "I suppose so," he answered, trying not to sound *too* impressed.

The smaller bat tugged at his wing. "Come on." They made their way down the woven path, which swayed and stretched under their feet. The giddy, happy feeling flooded through Koa, and he barely suppressed an urge to bounce on the flexible walkway.

The path led to a sort of wide, rounded hill at the center of the treetop, and above that hill, the Kites hovered. Koa stared up at them. Before now, he had only ever seen them from afar: tiny, brightly-colored shapes that spun and dipped and twisted in the sky above neighboring Kingdoms. This close, they proved to be enormous: seven diamonds of multicolored fabric, each looking large enough to shelter Koa's home. They hovered high above, placid in the calm wind, changing their drifting direction as the breeze shifted east or north. Their surface was calligraphed with runes and letters that were indecipherable to Koa. Flying foxes who knew how to read the kites could get all kinds of information from them: temperature, wind direction and speed, humidity, and even what the weather would be a day from now.

Maiel climbed to the top of the hill and waved to Koa. "Come up here. You've got to try this."

Koa followed after him. At the top of the hill, he had to duck under a thin cable that ran around the perimeter, looping under constraining branches. All the Kites were attached to the cable by their own thick cords, and it was these that he found most fascinating. The ropes were so finely and carefully woven that he could not see how they were constructed, and they showed no signs of stress or rot or damage. They were attached to the perimeter cable not by knots but by loops that let them slide freely back and forth. He ran his fingers across the surface of one and found it smooth and finely grained. "This is remarkable," he said. "These ropes must be nearly unbreakable. What are they made of?"

"I don't know," Maiel answered with a puzzled expression. "They're just rope."

Koa flushed at having been caught fascinated by something so simple. "But if the Lower Kingdoms had it, just think—no more deathly falls from a ladder breaking or a strand snapping. No more smashed shipments or houses coming apart. With rope like this you could fish for crocs."

Maiel gave him an appraising stare. "I guess you're right. It's so easy to take even the little things for granted up here. We don't really know how good we have it, do we?"

Koa shrugged his wings, feeling embarrassed.

"Come here." Maiel waved a wing. "Come and stand right… here." He pointed down at his feet.

"Okay." Koa moved forward uncertainly, toward the center of the broad platform, the flexible mesh of the woven branches giving him a bouncy gait. He stopped a few feet from Maiel.

"Come on," Maiel said with a smile, waving. "Right up here. Trust me."

Koa came closer, stepping up until he was nearly pressed against Maiel. "Okay, but I don't see what—" He broke off with a gasp as a strange feeling broke through him. It was like a fire blazing inside him, igniting all his senses. The breeze licked at his fur, the wood beneath his feet was cool and smooth and coarse and sturdy. He became lost in the present; his memories evaporated like water on the hearth, and all thoughts of his future became incomprehensible. The moment was all that existed—him standing there, Maiel against him, and a terrific energy that nearly lifted him from his toes. He felt in that moment that he could do anything, that nothing was impossible.

"You feel it?" Maiel whispered.

"What is it?" He was too overwhelmed to worry about sounding ignorant anymore.

"It's the heart of the Kingdom's magic. The roots soak it up out of the seawater. The Kingdom pulls it up into its wood, helping it to grow strong, and focuses it upward like a beam of light. All the sorcerers' strongest spells are performed right here, in the heart of magic. Do you like it?"

Koa shuddered at the feeling. "It's amazing."

Maiel pressed himself against Koa's chest and leaned up, smiling at him. There was sweet honey on his breath.

Koa dipped his head down and tasted it. Maiel's lips were warm and soft against his. He folded his wings about Maiel and squeezed him close, feeling the slender flying fox yield against him. The soft tickle of a tongue fluttered into his mouth, and he brushed his own against it.

Then Maiel pulled him forward, out of the flow of magic, and the wildfire blazing within him faded into embers, the energy that had crackled at his fingertips gone, and there was only the embrace, the cool of the night breeze in his fur. Memories returned, anticipation, worries, and the strange lightheadedness he'd had all evening, but through all these the kiss persisted, and he tilted his head and kissed back with new passion, his fingers sliding down Maiel's slender sides to his hips.

Maiel broke it first, breathing heavily. "You're very strong," he whispered, his wings against Koa's chest. "Stronger than you look."

"I, uh, I fly a lot."

Maiel giggled at that, though Koa had no idea why.

He leaned back a little, wanting to feel that electrifying rush of magic again. "Why is it so quiet?" he wondered. "Why don't other people come up here to try this?"

"Oh, well, we're not really supposed to. It's not good to stand in the flow too long. It makes you want it all the time. Besides, only people who can use magic can feel it."

Koa nearly protested that he couldn't use any magic at all, but then remembered the enchantment that shrouded him. Perhaps that was why he had felt it. "What made you think I would feel anything?"

Maiel's eyes twinkled. "A lucky guess, maybe."

"Well, I haven't had any training. Have you? Your father's a sorcerer, isn't he?"

Withdrawing from Koa's wings, the smaller bat nodded stiffly. "Yes, he is. But I don't want to study magic. Not when all I'd ever get to do is entertain the Upper Kingdoms or keep the lower classes out. I'd rather practice law. That's all about trying to make things fair. Or at least it's supposed to be."

"But magic benefits everyone, not just the flying foxes. Poor folk use glowlamps same as the rich."

"True, but do they ever have anything like that?" Maiel nodded back at the Firefly Ball. "Does anyone spellweave their houses for them, or protect their children from disease, or conjure cold drinks on hot days?"

"Not really." Koa was surprised at the questions. He hadn't realized how much magic did for the flying foxes, how different their lives truly were.

Maiel sighed. "Anyway, no matter how good I got at magic, I'd always be a disappointment compared to my father, the great Toller the Magician."

For Koa, the words seemed to wake him from a pleasant half-sleep. Toller. Toller the Magician. This whole night had a price, and he'd very nearly forgotten it. "Toller?" he repeated numbly.

"You've heard of him, I see. I'm not too surprised."

"No, wait. I had a—" He patted at his clothes, suddenly frightened. Where had he put the parcel?

"Are you all right?" Maiel peered at him.

"My cloak! Where did I put my cloak?"

"You weren't wearing one when I met you. Strange sort of thing to wear, isn't it? Not so good for flight."

No, he'd taken it off. He'd given it to the coat check. And that was where the parcel was now. "I'm so sorry, Maiel. I just remembered something I need to take care of. It's urgent."

"Right now? Will you back?" Maiel asked, sounding disappointed.

"Er, I don't know. Maybe." He looked up at the sky, trying to judge the time. The moon was almost directly overhead. He looked back at Maiel, and then, as though cued by the goddess of fate herself, felt a tingling in the tips of his ears. The enchantment was wearing off.

He stumbled backward, reaching up to feel the tips of his ears. Did it already show? How could it be past midnight already? He hadn't even heard the bell.

"Is something wrong?" Maiel's tone shifted from dismay to concern.

He flattened his ears backward, hiding them from view as the tingling crept lower. If he didn't deliver that parcel, Ruduuk would be furious. And he'd saddle Koa with a debt it would take years, if not decades, to pay off. But that parcel was a down below, in a room full of hundreds of dancing bats, and magical lights that hid behind wings and illuminated them. It might as well be on the other side of the ocean.

"No, no, everything's all right," he said, trying to force a care-free laugh into his tone. "Ha, ha, ha. I just—I really need to go. I'm so sorry."

He could ignore it. Just let the enchantment wear off, hurry back down and get the package. But then everyone would see him. They'd stare. They'd laugh. And worse, *Maiel* would see him. He couldn't let that happen, not when everything had been going so well. Not after that kiss.

The tingling moved down his face. Any moment now, Maiel would be able to notice it. He spun around, scanning the treetop, and with his back to Maiel, asked, "Is there any other way down from here besides the way we came?"

"I don't think so. Not unless you want to fly. Listen, are you sure everything is okay? You're acting very strange. Maybe I can help."

Koa nearly turned back, but the tingling moved down over his muzzle. However fine his features had looked before, they would not be so appealing now. He hurried down the hill and toward the rim of the pathway, looking over the edge. The darkness of the Beards yawned below—the party and inhabited areas must be some distance away. There were no lights of houses here, nor whirling fireflies. *You must not attempt to fly*, Ruduuk had warned him. But what other choice did he have? The spell had worn off all the way down to his neck, now. Soon it would reach his wings, and he would be trapped.

"Goodbye, Maiel," he called. "I very much enjoyed our time."

"Will I see you again soon?" Maiel hurried down the hill after him.

"I promise. Tomorrow! Look for me tomorrow!" The tingling had reached the tops of his limbs, now, and he could feel the awful numbness of the tears forming in the membranes once more. It was now or never.

He stretched his wings, held his breath, and stepped over the edge of the pathway. "Wait!" he heard Maiel call, and then his stomach wrenched away and he was tumbling in circles. He flapped his wings desperately, but he could neither tell which way was up, nor how to move those wings to right himself. Panic seized him; he flailed with his wings, but only spun himself around. The grey night world and looming shapes of the Beards careened before his eyes. Then time slowed.

He saw the glitter of moonlight on the waves down below, and the pale circles of glowlamps. His feet reached down instinctively, his head stretched upward. His wings beat once, and he felt himself rise. He flapped again and bounced higher on the air. He had time for one gasp of elation before the holes in his wings tore anew, ripping open painfully, and then he dropped toward the waves below. He felt the rippling resistance of the barrier as he fell through it, and closed his eyes, waiting for the impact of a branch or house or murky sea to end him. Stupid. He'd been stupid to try to fly.

He struck something coarse; lines of it dug into his face and side. He bounced into the air a few feet and then fell again heavily, one leg slipping through a circle of rope. The Nets had caught him.

He lay in their rude embrace for a while, his heart fluttering in his chest. The strips of torn flesh that made up his wings hung through the gaps in the rope mesh. Alive. He was alive. And in love. And in terrible, staggering debt.

The world of the flying foxes still flickered and shone above him, still thrummed with the sounds of the music. He had to get back there. Somehow, some way, he had to get back.

Chapter 8

L ook, I don't even know how it happened," Koa stammered. The slitted eyes of Ruduuk were fixed on him with a malevolent fury. "I think it wore off in less than four hours. I never heard the midnight bell!"

"You never heard the bell because you were carousing instead of doing your mudding job!" Ruduuk roared, his needle-teeth snapping inches away from Koa's face. "Plenty of time for loud music. Plenty of time for dancing. Time for lovely magical lights and sweet wine and basking in pools with pretty girls, eh? But no time to deliver one simple parcel. Well, you'll come to regret it, won't you, you little swamp rat?"

"Oi, that's offensive," Tug complained loudly. "And how do you know what goes on at those balls anyhow?"

Ruduuk ignored him. "Well, where is it? Where did you leave it? What happened?"

Koa shook his head miserably. "I left it in my cloak at the coat check. Then the spell wore off and I couldn't get back to it."

"At the coat check," Ruduuk groaned. "You wretched, idiotic little halfwit. And anyone might have found it there, anyone. You've ruined me. You've ruined all my plans."

"Maybe no one saw it," Koa offered. "Maybe it's still there, and they're wondering why I never came back to get it."

"Or maybe they were immediately alerted to its presence when the enchantment faded and your mudding cloak mudding disappeared!" Ruduuk bellowed. With one mighty swipe of a taloned paw, he swept the contents of one counter across the room, enchanted toys and knick-knacks dashing against the wall and scattering across the floor.

"Hey, you break it, you bought it," Tug said helpfully.

Ruduuk snorted into his face, teeth clenched, and for a moment, Koa was afraid the hedge lizard was about to rake at his brother's face.

"Look, I'm really sorry. I made a mistake. But I can get it right. Give me one more spray of the Eau de Grâce. I'll go up right away. I'll find it, deliver it, and come back to you. Please? Give me a chance?"

Ruduuk leaned back against the wall, his breathing steadily slowing and calming. He pressed his lips together as if considering, and then, in a more measured voice, asked, "And why should I give you anything?"

Koa hunched lower, drawing his wings close to his sides. "Because I'm sorry? Because we've been doing business with you for years, and it's only one mistake?"

"Ah yes, business." Ruduuk looked down his scaled snout at the two of them. "I'm afraid that's quite finished."

Tug put his paws up. "Hold on, hold on, what do you mean, finished? You mean like—"

"I mean that I bought salvage from the both of you as a favor, a kindness, one that I no longer have any wish to extend. I will purchase nothing from either of you until your debt is repaid. One thousand rupiah, I believe you agreed."

"But that's not fair!" Koa shouted. "How are we supposed to pay it back if you're not buying any salvage off of us?"

Ruduuk scowled. "That's hardly my concern. You should have considered that before you reneged on our deal."

"But look, not allowin' us to pay you back ain't that clever, is it?" Tug said. "Be mad at Koa all you want, but let him work off his debt. Or let him try to go and nick yer old box back. Something. No reason to just be stupid about it."

Koa winced.

"Stupid?" Ruduuk showed all his fangs, yellow and serrated. "You dare to call me stupid, you barely coherent pugilistic dollop of swamp slime?" He lunged toward Tug, who turned nimbly out of the way. Ruduuk fell, his heavy body dropping so heavily it made the shop shudder, his chin striking against the floor. He pushed himself up with his short arms, red eyes furious slits. "Get out," he hissed at them. "Get out of my shop. And don't come back until you have the money!"

Koa seized Tug's paw before the otter could try compounding his mistake and yanked him toward the door. Ruduuk charged after them on all fours, his massive body twisting sinuously around the counters. He slammed the door behind them.

Panting in fright, Koa sat down on the edge of the footpath and put his head in his wings. What were they going to do?

"Well," Tug said, strolling past him, paws folded behind his back, "someone put too much salt in his stew this morning."

"How can you be so cavalier about this?" Koa muttered into the tent of his wings.

"Cavalier what? Sensible, right? Because there ain't no use in getting all gloomy now. Besides, I've been in worse scrapes than this."

"Like what?"

"Like the other day when a croc thought he might use me for a toothpick, eh? Or, you know, back when I ran with the LTSL, near every day."

Koa rolled his eyes. "That's different."

"Course it is. Everything's different. Doesn't mean it's not a *little* bit the same, though."

"You don't understand. I promised Maiel I'd come back tonight. I swore it!"

Tug blinked at him, his beady eyes incomprehensible. "Did you? Well. Wouldn't worry too much about it. Nobody takes drunken promises too serious."

"I wasn't drunk!" Koa protested.

"Oi, when you came home last night I thought your breath was going to peel the wallpaper. You were sotted as an old persimmon."

Koa started to argue, but then recalled the odd light-headedness he'd felt all night, the foolish way he'd behaved. Alcohol was rare in the Lower Kingdoms. Could he really have been drunk? That would explain how he could have forgotten the parcel so easily. He wondered if perhaps Ruduuk would accept that excuse by way of apology. But no, of course he wouldn't. At least not now. The hedge lizard was furious. Perhaps he would calm down later.

"Still, I want to keep the promise. I *need* to," Koa admitted.

Tug shrugged, and padded down the footpath toward their boat. "Nothing stopping you. You can head on up there any time you like. Go and see him. Tell him the truth."

"You know I can't do that," Koa said. He followed after Tug, folding his wings close to his sides.

Chapter 9

The first thing Koa saw upon entering the hideout was a surprisingly large pile of salvage heaped up in the center of the floor. Tarnished metal and cut glass glittered in the shining heap perched atop a little pyramid of oysters. "You went out diving without me?"

Tug gave him a feeble grin. "Surprise. Did it while you were conked out recovering from your night of splendiferous whatnots."

"That was dangerous, Tug! Supposing the croc had come back."

"Aw, he's puttered off to calmer waters. Ones without so many mouthfuls of sticks and rope. Anyway, I had Demel looking out for me in the boat."

"You could have waited." Koa made the protest, though he didn't much feel it. His mind and stomach were clenched around the impossible situation.

Tug flopped into a creaky hammock, using his stumped tail to rock himself back and forth. "When you went off, I figured it like, either A, he's goin' to come back here and everything's gone swimmingly, in which case he'll be glum as scum about not bein' able to go back, or two, everything will have gone awful, and he'll need somethin' to distract himself. And what do you know, I'm so mudding clever, I was right on both counts."

With one taloned toe, Koa nudged the pile of salvage, and it collapsed across the floor in a mucky puddle. "Not like it'll do us any good now. We might as well toss it all back in the ocean."

"Aw, don't be like that. Jilly over in the Bearded's Toes will still give us something for the mess. Not a lot, but something. And with that and the rupiah you get from mendin' ladders and my fishing, we'll come up with something in time."

Koa shrugged. "I guess." He wondered if Maiel was looking for him yet, waiting for him, wondering why he hadn't shown up. He stared out at the sky. The sun was already sinking toward the sea.

"Cheer up, Breezy. We'll pay that bag of scales back somehow. You'll see. Things will go back to normal in no time."

"I don't *want* them to go back to normal!" Koa heard the frustration rising in his voice, but didn't care to stop it. "This sucks, Tug. Trawling the roots for the garbage that my people couldn't even be bothered to hold onto, begging for just enough to get a taste of their life here and there? I'm sick of it. I hate it."

Tug sat up in the hammock. "I kinda thought you liked our life. I like it."

"It was fine when we were pups. But we're grown up now, and we're still doing this? For how long? Is this going to be our whole lives?"

"There's still the oysters. We'll find that pearl."

Koa sputtered. "Oh, for—for the love of mud, Tug!" He kicked the pile of oysters, sending them scattering across the floor. "Don't you get it? There's not going to be any pearl! It's just a stupid fantasy. It's a pup's dream. We could dig up all the oysters in the Kingdoms and not find one mudding pearl. And even if we did, so what? It's just one pearl. How much do you think that's worth? You think you can buy a new house for our whole family? When I was up there"—he pointed toward the treetops—"I saw people wearing whole strings of them. Maybe fifty of them at once! And they don't own a whole Arm of a Kingdom. They're just average bats living their average lives, out for a good time at the ball. You really think finding one stupid pearl would make a difference?"

Tug's eyes were wide and liquid. "It might."

"It won't. We'll eat well for a week or two, maybe get some new clothes or some new furniture, and then everything will be back to normal. This big idea of yours of finding a pearl and changing all our lives is just a stupid dream. No matter what happens, I'll always be here, torn wings, an outcast, lonely."

"I didn't know you were that lonely." The otter's voice was almost inaudible.

Koa sat down heavily on the floor. One leg sprawled in the puddle of muck from the salvage, but he didn't care. He rested his head in his wings. "Up there, there's a bat who's waiting for me right now. Who liked me. Who kissed me. I promised him I'd come back. I *promised* him. And he's so sweet, Tug, and so nice, and so handsome, and all I want in the world is just to be back up there with him right now."

He heard the hammock creak as Tug got to his feet. "Look, I dunno what you thought was gonna happen. This big plan of yours, I never really understood it. You wanted to go up to this big party and get this fella of yours to fall in love with some other guy whose skin you wore. I didn't see the point. But it was your dream, right? Who am I to call it stupid?"

His voice lowered. "Well my dreams ain't stupid either, little brother. They're an ocean and a half too pretty for me, and maybe they're impossible, but that's what makes 'em worth followin'. And I thought"—he sighed—"I thought they were *ours*. I thought we shared 'em."

"Well, you were wrong," Koa said bitterly. He regretted it as soon as he said it, but he couldn't bring himself to take it back. The days of fishing in the afternoon sun and counting up their treasures had been fond memories, but next to the glamor and flash of the Firefly Ball, they seemed foolish and embarrassing. Just two ignorant yokels grubbing around in the muck for faded trinkets, talking about how they were going to strike it rich. When he thought of it, his ears burned with shame. How could Maiel ever be impressed with something like that, whole wings or no?

Tug opened his muzzle to reply, then snapped it closed, giving Koa a considering stare. "You don't mean it," he decided. "You just need some kip and a full belly and you'll feel better. You'll see. I ain't givin' up on our plans and you won't either. We'll get it all sorted out."

Koa looked out the door at the setting sun and thought of Maiel waiting, up there at the top of the Kingdom, where they'd kissed and the magic had flowed through him like a lightning bolt. "Just leave me alone."

"All right." Tug stepped through the scattered pile of salvage, careful not to crush any of it under his webbed toes, as though every piece were precious. "I'm heading back. I'll tell Mum to set a place for you. We'll all be waiting."

Koa nodded, and the otter left. Once he was gone, Koa crawled to the edge of the doorway and sat, watching the sun melt into red blobs as it sank below the horizon. "Stupid," he muttered to himself. "Stupid." He wasn't sure what he meant. Tug. Himself. Ruduuk. The whole situation. But Tug had been right, of course. What had he been thinking, going up to the

Crown and getting Maiel to fall for some dumb magical disguise? He hadn't been thinking at all, of course. He had just wanted to see him, to see the Ball, to taste it. Like a taste could ever be enough. He got to his feet, pacing. Why had he forgotten all the rules as soon as he'd gone up there? Why hadn't he told Maiel the truth?

If he had to do it over, if he had just one more night, he could make it all right. He could deliver Ruduuk's parcel, and tell Maiel who he really was. He wasn't sure how the flying fox would react—if he would understand, or get mad, or what, but it was better than this.

It was too late anyway. That avenue was gone. Even if he went back to Maiel the next day, torn wings and all, would the bat even believe him? Who could ever think that the graceful, charming, elegant creature of the night before could be this *crippled* thing?

His mind skipped over the word, repulsed by it. Never call yourself that. His mother had always told him that in harsh terms, when a shopkeeper or a passerby, or, gods forbid, one of his siblings had dared use it. That's not what you are. The things that happen to you don't define you. And he had never really thought of himself that way. His wings had never really bothered him. Not unless he dared venture toward the flying foxes. Flying was in their name. It was what they were. He knew they could never accept him.

And neither could Maiel. It was as simple as that. There was no use grieving over it. No use getting angry. It was just an unpleasant fact of life, to be swallowed down like the part of a meal that was nasty but good for you.

The thought of a meal made his stomach pang, and he considered the warm light of a dinner table and a room full of rowdy siblings who couldn't give two flaps about what his wings were like nor how crude he was. It sounded a lot better than sitting in a musty old hollow that stank of stagnant seawater. He got to his feet and turned to go.

As he did, the sunlight caught a glimmer across the room. Something on the floor shone. He frowned, wondering what it could be; it didn't look like the tarnished brass or silver of the salvage. He crossed the room and picked up a dark grey oyster shell, one of the ones he had kicked against the wall. It had struck with such force that the shell had fragmented, shards of coarse, ridged calcium embedded in the white flesh of the oyster. This was going to stink tomorrow if he didn't get rid of it. He pulled up the broken corner of the shell, and froze.

Inside was a glistening, silky-white marble. Disbelieving, he pulled away more of the shell and lifted the thing out into his fingers. It was heavier than it looked. It was also the biggest pearl he'd ever seen, as big around as his thumb.

He could hardly breathe. He turned to run home, eager to tell Tug what he had found—what *they* had finally found—a pearl like no other. He wondered what it was worth. Ten thousand rupiah? More? It was possible. It would also pay off his debt to Ruduuk, ten times over—which would be worth nine more sprays from the bottle. Nine more nights to visit Maiel, to win him over.

Even with only one more dose of the Eau de Grâce, Koa could deliver Ruduuk's parcel and pay off his debt. It would be like getting another night of enchantment for free.

He bit his lip, agonizing. His family would be sitting around the dinner table now, wondering where he was. But Maiel would be waiting too, and Koa had promised he'd be there. And there would be no point explaining this to Tug. Tug wouldn't understand. Tug would just argue.

No, Koa decided. With one last visit to the Upper Kingdoms, he could fix everything. He closed his tattered wing around the pearl.

Chapter 10

Ruduuk!" He hammered on the hedge lizard's door, though it wasn't really a door at all. When the shop was closed, the doorway just grew itself together, as though there had never been an opening at all. "Ruduuk, open up!"

For a while there was no response, but he kept pounding, and when that didn't work, he began kicking at the smooth surface, until the lizard's red eyes appeared at the little window near the top.

"Go away, you little pest! There's nothing you can say or do to change my mind."

Koa held the pearl up to the window and heard the lizard hiss.

Then the opening melted apart with a noise like paper being crumpled. Ruduuk hunched in the opening, silhouetted by the light of a few small glowlamps behind him. "Do come in," he purred, stepping to one side.

Koa shuffled past him, blinking in the light of the shop. He kept the pearl gripped tightly in one wing.

The doorway grew closed once more, and Ruduuk hefted himself past Koa and settled behind his counter, interlacing his fingers. "I'm surprised to see you here so late, and without your… accomplice." Koa looked at the floor. "Ah. I believe I understand. No need to explain. You're like me. You know what it takes to get what you want."

"It's not like that," Koa began.

"Of course it isn't, of course," Ruduuk said, doing his best at a soothing tone. "You're here to right past wrongs, is all. You're here to do what's best for everyone. Isn't that right?"

"That's right." Koa had actually been thinking exactly that, but coming from Ruduuk, the words sounded wrong, somehow. Venomous.

"Let us see what you've brought, then." The lizard spread his talons across the counter.

Hesitantly, Koa opened his fingers and let the milky marble clatter out onto the counter. In the warm, orange light of the glowlamps it blushed like the rising sun.

Ruduuk hissed again, his red eyes glittering greedily. "A lovely specimen. Not the finest I've seen, to be sure, but a rare find all the same. You can consider your debt repaid, boy."

"Now wait a minute." Koa snatched the pearl up again, and the look of dismay that flashed across Ruduuk's face told him all he needed to know. "It's worth far more than a thousand rupiah. I don't have to sell this to you. Maybe I should see what other merchants think it's worth."

"Ten thousand!" Ruduuk shouted, and snatched at his closed fingers.

He stepped back, startled that the lizard would have raised his price so high so quickly. "Fifty," he countered, and felt a shiver of thrill at his own daring.

Ruduuk's eyes narrowed, and then he relaxed, settling back behind his counter, chuckling. "Dear boy, you overplay your hand. Fifty thousand? You've no idea what it's worth, do you? You're flying blind now."

"Then perhaps I should take it to another merchant after all. I can pay you back easily enough with what they give me, can't I?"

The lizard half-climbed across the counter. "They will not value it half as much as I! Twenty thousand!"

"Thirty five."

Ruduuk bared his razor teeth. "Thirty."

Koa hesitated. Any other day, he'd have taken the pearl around, have it checked out. But then, any other day, Tug would be here with him. They'd be celebrating. And tonight, Maiel was waiting. He held his breath. "Thirty," he said finally. "And you *give* me another spray from the bottle and a new parcel so I can finish the errand and pay off my debt." That was fair, he thought. It was better this way. Tug would have only annoyed the lizard and driven the price down.

A grin split Ruduuk's face. "Ah, so that's it, is it? That's your price? Fair enough then, boy, fair enough. You're too clever a negotiator for this old shopkeeper. Thirty it is. And a bonus enchantment. You have a deal." He held out his hand.

Koa's heart sank. The hedge lizard looked far too pleased with himself to have paid a fair price. He could hardly back down now, though. He took Ruduuk's scaly fingers in his own.

The lizard clasped them tight. "The rupiah to be paid after delivery of the parcel. Agreed?" Koa nodded uneasily. Ruduuk shook his wing. "Good. Wait here." His hand passed over the surface of the counter, and then the pearl was gone.

"Wait," Koa cried, but Ruduuk ignored him, stooping as he bustled toward the back of the shop and vanished.

So that was it. Thirty thousand and another chance to see Maiel. He sighed and went to the window, staring out at the winking night. What would Tug say when he found out? Something joyful, he told himself firmly. Tug would be happy that they were rich. Nothing else would matter. He lodged the thought firmly in the front of his mind and tried to ignore the sick feeling settling in his stomach.

"So eager to get going?" Ruduuk's voice came from behind him, startling him.

He turned to see the monitor lizard standing at the counter, a package wrapped in brown paper tucked under one arm.

"I just want to pay off this debt for good."

Ruduuk gave him a calculating stare. "Good. Good. So, tell me again, what are you to do?"

"Take the parcel to the house of Toller the Magician."

"And whom do you deliver it to?"

He paused. "Toller?"

Ruduuk shook his head. "No one. You make sure the package is delivered inside his house. Be very careful. If the parcel I gave you before was discovered, his enemies may be watching. It is better not to let anyone see you. What are you not to do?"

"Stand near a mirror, get seawater on me, or try to fly?"

Ruduuk growled. "What else?"

Koa hesitated. Had there been other rules that he'd forgotten? "Er—"

He almost yelped as the lizard gripped his muzzle in a surprisingly strong hand. "You are not to do *anything* else. You are to go to the Crown and deliver the parcel. Because if you do not, your pearl is mine, and you receive no payment. You will owe me two thousand, not one. And this debt I will levy upon you and your whole family. Do you understand?"

The grip around his muzzle made nodding impossible. "Yes," he managed.

All at once, Ruduuk let him go, relaxing into an easy smile. "Good. I'm pleased that we have agreement." He put the parcel into Koa's trembling wings and began ushering him toward the doorway.

"But wait, the—"

"Ah, yes the enchantment, of course." With his tail, he lifted the bottle of opalescent liquid from its hiding place behind the counter. Koa barely had time to close his eyes before the lizard spritzed him in the face with it. "You had better go," Ruduuk said. "The moonlight is waiting."

With a crumpling sound, the wooden wall of the tree pulled back. Ruduuk gave Koa a shove, sending him stumbling out into the moonlight.

Whereas before, the magic had changed him inch by inch with the rising moon, like settling slowly into a hot bath, this time it transformed him all at once, like plunging into one. It swallowed him in a full-body tingle and bone-deep ache. The sensation was unpleasant and disorienting, but it was over quickly. He looked down to see the fine clothes around his limbs again, the softer fur on his arms and legs, and his wings, whole and perfect.

He headed forward and stopped still. Tug was standing a little ways down the footpath, under a glowlamp.

"Koa?" the otter called, peering in the dim light. He scurried forward. "Thank the Twelve! No one knew what had happened to you. I was sure I'd find you knockin' about the hideout, but you weren't—" He faltered. "You got magicked up again."

Koa held out the parcel. "Ruduuk gave me another chance. He said he'll cancel the debt if I deliver it."

"Gave?" Tug eyed him suspiciously. "What do you mean he gave it? Ruduuk don't give anything that ain't a poke in the eye. How'd you pay for it? You didn't go getting yourself into more trouble than before, did you? You get a loan from that dodgy old Hooka down in the Shallows?"

"N—no, I…" He couldn't think of an answer, and shrugged his wings.

Tug frowned at him, and then his eyes went wide, his whiskers drooping. "It was the smashed-in oyster, weren't it? The one with the pieces all over the floor. Nicked my paw on it but good."

Koa looked away.

"We found one, didn't we? After grubbing around in the roots for years, we finally found one. And you didn't even come tell me."

More than the time the croc had Tug up against the tree trunk, more than when Koa stepped off the Crown before Maiel could see him change back, more than any other time in his life, Koa wished he could fly. If he could, he would fly away now and never look back. But he could only stand with his back to Ruduuk's shop and stammer at his brother. "Tug, believe me, I was—I was gonna tell you, tomorrow. I just thought that—"

"So it's true?" Tug came closer, dismay written across his face. "You—you didn't even come and tell me first. You just came straight here and got yourself pretty again for your boy upstairs. Right after you got done explainin' to me how all my dreams were stupid. And then you rowed off with 'em in your pocket."

Koa shrunk in on himself. "I just wanted to pay off the debt first."

"You coulda done that any time!" Tug shouted at him. "You coulda marched up there easy as you please and popped the package into that stuffy old sorcerer's paws or house or whatever it is. Anyway, you wanted to see that Maiel. And that you coulda done too, if you weren't such a coward."

"No, I couldn't!" Koa protested.

"Why not? Because they woulda said mean things to you?"

"Because I got a letter!"

Whatever he'd been about to shout next, Tug swallowed it down. "What? What do you mean, you got a letter?"

Koa sighed. "He sent me a letter the next day. He said it was better if I didn't come."

Tug looked like whatever he'd swallowed had tasted especially nasty. "Well then he—then he's rotten. And who cares what he thinks? Why should you? He sends you off just because one of his mudding stuck-up friends thinks it's funny to mock you in front of the group—"

"No, it's not like that! He's sweet and kind. You'd like him. Only I think he was afraid of what would happen if I went up there like—like me. Maybe what the other bats would do."

Tug snorted and shook his head. "I dunno why you want anything to do with any of 'em. But I guess it's a big deal to you, eh? Enough that you'd… you'd…"

Koa looked up toward the Crown of the Great Drinker. "You can't imagine what it's like, Tug. To go walking around them like you're one of them. Nobody stares. Nobody makes faces. Nobody makes a big show of *not* looking at you. Nobody cares who or what you are. It's like going home."

"No, it ain't."

"What?"

Tug folded his short arms across his chest. "If that's what you think, then you don't know what home is. It ain't where nobody cares. Home is where what you are and who you are *matters*."

Koa sighed. "That's easy for you to say. You don't have giant, disgusting scars or torn webs so you can't swim."

"Got a stumpy tail."

"It's not the same."

Tug shrugged.

"I have to go," Koa said. "I don't have all night." He sidled past his older brother, who stepped aside, slumping miserably. On his way to the boat he turned back. "Tug, listen, I'm—I'm really sorry."

"Was it pretty?" Tug asked in a sad, plaintive voice.

"Was what?"

"The pearl. Was it pretty? I woulda liked to have seen it, at least. Held it in my paw. Just once."

It was one of the most beautiful things I've ever seen. Koa could think of nothing to say that wouldn't hurt Tug worse, and so he just turned and hurried down toward the docks. The rising night breezes catching in his untorn wings nearly took him off his feet.

Chapter 11

Koa climbed the footways of the Bearded Kingdom, surefooted and graceful once more, the fine silks of his conjured clothing rustling in the wind. The scent of the enchantment still clung to his fur, chemical and sickly-sweet, like rotting flowers.

He ascended through the barrier that guarded the world of the flying foxes, and higher, until he stopped finally to rest, gazing down at the Nets. The sight of them made him wince. His neck still ached and his limbs smarted from the bruises he'd received falling into them the night before. He shouldn't have tried to fly. That had been dumb. He'd done a *lot* of dumb things last night. But he was putting them all right now. He was going to fix everything.

That would have to include Maiel, he reminded himself. What would he tell him? How would he explain his sudden disappearance last night? What could he say to be able to see him not only tonight, but on other nights? *You don't* have *to fix that tonight*, a quiet side of him suggested. *You could use the money for more enchantments, and buy a fortnight of visits. Better yet, save them for the Firefly Balls, and meet him every week for months.*

He toyed with the idea for a while, but every time, the betrayed look on his brother's face resurfaced in his mind. He couldn't think about Tug right now, so he shoved those considerations away. Better to talk to Maiel tonight and have done with it.

Hi, Maiel. Listen, there's something you need to know. I lied to you about everything—about my name, about who I was and where I was from and what I look like. I actually tricked you and all the other bats here with a spell I got from the hedge lizard. No. That wasn't going to work.

Hi, Maiel. Sorry, I know it's difficult to explain, but I can never see you again. But maybe you'd like my friend Koa. He's a lot like me. I bet you two would hit it off. But look, maybe you'd be better off visiting him down in the Lower Kingdoms in his tiny house with fourteen otters running around.

He sighed. There was no good way to explain it. Nothing would work. Maybe goodbye was the only thing left to say. Maybe this was a dream that was just not his to chase. Maybe all his prospects lay down at the bottom of the Drowned Kingdom, crushed under the fallen Atlas.

No. That was Tug's voice in his head. Stubborn, relentlessly hopeful Tug. *You want it, you hold onto it. You chase after it. You don't let none of them stuck-up bats stand in your way. If it's near to you, makes you reach for it when you ain't even tryin', then you don't let it go that easy, Breezy. Ha! I'm a poet and don't know it.*

"I guess I'll just have to figure out what to say when I get there," he decided. And he climbed.

When he reached the Head, he was surprised at all the activity. It was far busier than he'd seen it or any other place—other than the Firefly Ball—at this time of night. Of course, he reminded himself, flying foxes were nocturnal. It was only due to his own family's schedule that he slept at night, but he often found himself drowsy during the day, and his rests at night fitful. Nights were when he ought to be awake, like his people.

They hurried back and forth, running errands, visiting shops, or idled around intersections in groups, chatting loudly, sipping hot beverages from thin bark cups or sinking their fangs into ripe fruit. For a moment, all Koa could do was stand and stare at the world of his kind who bustled around above his head at a time when he normally slept. He felt as though he had been sleeping his whole life, missing everything of any importance.

He took a deep breath, and reminded himself of the parcel under his wing. He could not afford to be distracted and make the mistake of last night again.

"Excuse me," he said, waving one wing toward a passing bat, who was hurrying by, pushing some kind of covered cart in front of him. It had wheels, but seemed to ignore gravity, traveling at rather steep angles without sliding.

"Yes, what is it?" the flying fox asked, brushing an arm across his forehead distractedly. Three infant heads poked up from the cart and squeaked at Koa.

He gave them a shy waggle of his wing-fingers. "Do you know where I might find the residence of Toller the Magician?"

"It's up in the Crown, of course," the flying fox said irritably. He took a pocket-watch from his waistcoat, gave it a baleful stare, and snapped it closed again. "Covered with lilacs. Gaudy thing. You can't miss it."

"Thank you," Koa began, but the flying fox had already set off.

"Bye-bye," peeped one of the pups in the perambulator, waving a wing. "Bye-bye!" they all chimed in as they were bustled away.

He waved back to them, and unbidden, stirred up old memories of being carried around by his mother during the cool, comforting night, staring up at passing strangers who were tall and fascinating, and being too shy to call out to them.

The Crown, he reminded himself, and hurried on. He followed the crowd down the main thoroughfare through the Head of the Beards, joining their bustle and enjoying the way no one gawked at him as he moved with them down into the tangle where all the Arms that made up the Head joined with the trunk. Then he passed up the largest arm toward the treetop, where silver moonlight filtered down through the leaves.

While it was true no one gawked, he did catch a few sidelong glances, mostly from young females, but a few males here and there. Once or twice he looked back and caught them staring, and felt his cheeks flush hot with embarrased pleasure.

Tain't you they're starin' at, Tug nattered in the back of his mind. *Just a pretty picture you're holdin' up for them. Who cares if they like the picture? Ain't you.*

You don't understand, he thought back at Tug fiercely. You don't know what it's like to have someone even look in my direction like that. It makes me feel like a person.

He nodded to himself. All the same, the flush fled his cheeks, and the occasional fascinated stares weren't as enjoyable as before.

The traffic thinned as he climbed the long Arm, and then bottled up again as everyone used the loop to switch from standing to hanging. He waited his turn patiently, and then gripped the woven road in his toes, following it toward the Crown.

Looking up, he realized with surprise that this was the same area where the Firefly ball had been held the night before. He hardly recognized it without the dancing crowds and lights. He scanned the area, trying to see where the coat check had been. There, across the way, he could make out what he thought was the spiral ramp, but he couldn't see the little woven stand beneath it. In fact, it must not have been the same ramp, for there was a passage below it, a gaping hole that led deeper into the Head.

It was a reminder that however comfortable he might feel here, this world was still new and confusing to him. Small wonder he'd forgotten his errand so easily the night before.

At the top of the Arm, he found himself following only a few others—it seemed that not as many people were interested in visiting the Crown. He dropped to his feet once more and wandered out onto the branching paths. The open sky swung dizzyingly above him, filled with stars. He clenched at the road unconsciously with his toes, suddenly feeling as though he might drop out of the Crown and plummet endlessly into the night. Perhaps this was why fewer bats came up here; they preferred the comfort of their weight swinging from their feet. Last night, the open sky had not bothered him much, but then again, he'd been drunk, if Tug was to be believed. Koa was still doubtful on that point.

He scanned the broad expanse of the Crown: there, the hill with the circle of rope and the Kites, swaying and diving in the shifting winds; scattered about, tall branches with the homes of the wealthy built into them. Covered with lilacs, the bat had said.

Koa wandered the woven paths, scanning for it. He passed a home that looked like it had been hollowed deep into an Arm, with no telling how far down it went. Another glimmered in the moonlight, apparently made of liquid glass, or perhaps perpetually flowing water, though Koa could see nothing of the rooms inside.

Farther down the paths he saw a home that could only be Toller's: a rising whirl of rooms spiraling around one of the Beards' upstretched Arms. The rooms didn't appear to be covered with lilacs so much as *made* of them; the walls were formed of the delicate curve of enormous petals, and great stems arched upward from the rooms to join with the Arm of the Beards. Some of the rooms appeared to be crafted upside down, and in others, the petals had unfolded to form a dais, exposing their enclosures to the night sky. Atop one, the warm light of a glowlamp illuminated the soft purple of the petals, a comfortable-looking pile of pillows, and a series of gleaming brass cylinders that might have been a telescope. Koa couldn't understand why anyone would call such a home gaudy. He thought it was lovely, and undeniable proof of the power of the sorcerer who lived there.

He stretched out his shoulders, gripped his parcel firmly, and headed for the home. It took him several minutes to find the door, which proved to be situated just beneath the Crown rather than on top of it, further evidence of the flying foxes' preference for hanging rather than standing. He supposed all of the homes up here had their entries below the mesh pathways. Or, he considered, at their tops, so that their occupants might simply fly to their own doorsteps.

As that was no option for him, he headed down to the lower door and tugged with one foot at the bell rope. A sonorous tone sounded from somewhere within. He waited by the door, which was oddly ordinary compared to the rest of the home: just a flat slab of wood painted blue. No sound came from within, and he wondered with growing concern whether anyone was home.

Would he even be able to hear someone approaching from within those floral walls? Up close, they appeared just as smooth and delicate as from a distance. He leaned over to brush one with his fingers. The surface felt soft and delicate, as though with a firm push, he might tear through. The door opened as he was leaning over, and he straightened in surprise.

"Kawa?" Maiel leaned around the half-opened door, blinking behind his round glasses. He was dressed in only a light shirt and shorts, which nonetheless looked soft and silken and very expensive.

For a moment, Koa was confused. Yes. Kawa. That was the name he'd given Maiel. "I told you I'd come back." He gazed uncomfortably at Maiel for a moment before feeling the parcel dig into his wing, reminding him why he'd come. "Er, may I come in?"

Maiel stared back. "Of—of course." He stepped away from the door, spreading one wing to invite Koa inside. "I must admit, I didn't expect to see you. I'm… pleased to find you well."

The inside of the home was cool and well-lit, with a light current of air carrying the faint scent of lilac. Koa stepped inside and looked around, catching his first glimpse in memory of the inside of a flying fox's home. The main room of the house was high-ceilinged, perhaps thirty or forty feet, with curved openings—fashioned into the curving petal walls—leading to other rooms or hallways, all the way up to the top. The walls themselves were glossy-smooth, and the whole room reminded Koa a bit of a conch shell Tug had once brought up from the shallows, its throat shiny and blushing as it spiraled into hidden depths.

Near the top of the large room, a strange, elongated brass device made of hoops and gears spun and whirled silently in complicated and dizzying patterns. It must have been magical, for the moving parts left faint tracers of light in the air—blue, pink, and green.

To his dismay, Koa saw at once that this was a home for flying creatures only—there were no staircases to take him to any of the other rooms. The house was wide and open and almost completely inaccessible, although he did notice a couple of curved ladders extending up either side of the home. They were braided of fine black rope, and appeared more decorative than practical, as there were neither sags nor kinks in their cords to indicate anyone used them regularly.

At several levels over his head, long petals extended from the walls, forming daises on which there appeared to be tables and comfortable furniture to lie on, but if there were any way to access those besides flying, Koa couldn't see it. He took a deep breath, hoping beyond reason that Maiel would not suggest flying off to a private room together. "How—uh—why didn't you think I'd keep my promise?"

The smaller bat blinked at him. "Well… it was just that you dove off that branch so suddenly, and you'd had a bit to drink, and—and I just wasn't sure if you were okay. I mean, that's a risky move to pull even if…" He trailed off.

Koa frowned, puzzled. "Even if what?"

Maiel bit his lip. "Look, can we go somewhere and talk?" He did not sound like he was looking forward to the conversation.

Koa looked about the home doubtfully, wondering which of the many inaccessible rooms Maiel would invite him to, his mind scrambling for excuses as to why he could not.

"Not here," Maiel added. "Outside. Someplace quiet."

"Okay." Koa nodded, turned toward the door, and then remembered his parcel. "Er, is there somewhere I can leave this? It's for your father."

"My father?" The flying fox gave Koa a curious stare. "I… suppose there on the Pembroke would be fine." He pointed to a small, leafed, wooden table nestled up against the wall near one of the decorative ladders. It had several hefty books and papers strewn across it, and they all looked yellowed and dusty.

Koa set the parcel on it and felt a great burden lift from his shoulders. His debt was repaid, his task finally complete. Ruduuk had no hold over him. And Koa would have money enough to put a smile back on Tug's muzzle, hopefully.

He gave the inside of the magnificent home one last admiring glance and followed Maiel out the door. They traveled on foot—for which Koa was immensely grateful—across the Crown, past the Kites, and to the edge of the Beards, where one limb stretched out far over the water. Maiel was talkative, commenting on the weather and how lovely the moon was and how much he'd enjoyed the dance the other night and that he hoped Kawa was well. But it was plain that his mind was elsewhere, and he spoke of these things only as pleasantries.

They hung as they moved out onto the branch, and eventually Maiel stopped, swaying above water that glittered with reflected starlight. He was silent for so long that Koa thought he must have forgotten what he wanted to say.

Feeling awkward, he tried to start the conversation himself. "Look, if this is about how suddenly I had to leave last night—"

"Koa, I know it's you," Maiel blurted out.

Koa froze, struggling to accept what he'd just heard. "That's—that's—who's Koa?"

Maiel folded his wings tightly. "It's kind of obvious, really. I mean, you came to the basement door, Koa. There's all these little ways you move, little things you don't understand. When you first came up to me, I thought you were kind of an ass, and then I thought maybe you were just strange. But then, when we went to get drinks, I looked up and saw your reflection in the table."

Your reflection will show your true self. The drink tables. Koa remembered them now. Silver, highly polished. Early in the night, they'd been filled with glasses, but by the time he and Maiel had gone for drinks, far fewer had remained, leaving a clear enough space that anyone might have easily glanced up and seen him in the mirrored surface—shoddy clothes, torn wings, and all.

He stared down, grasping for words that might explain what he'd done. "Maiel, look, I only wanted to see you again so badly, and you'd told me not to come—"

"I… I did write that, didn't I?" Maiel hunched into his folded wings. "I told myself I wasn't going to be like *them*, with the barriers and the exclusion, and then I tried to keep you out, too. Only I thought—I was afraid that if you came, you'd get hurt again or cause some kind of row. It wasn't a good reason. It's them I should be standing against, not you. And I forced you to go to some cheap magician for a spell I bet you couldn't even afford, didn't I?"

"You didn't force me," Koa objected. "You were right. I wouldn't have dared to come, not as I—not with my wings like they are. And there probably would have been a scene. It wouldn't have been so nice a night.'

"Koa." Maiel gave him a curious stare. "Do you think you're the only fox around with torn wings?"

"Well, of course not, but I…" he trailed off. He hadn't really considered that there might be others like him in the Upper Kingdoms. "Are there a lot?"

"Well, not a crowd, but injuries happen. Foxes get caught in storms, blown into trees, injured in fights. Sometimes they simply fall. And some are just born wrong, you know? And when you get old enough, and your joints start wearing out…" Maiel shrugged. "The families take care of them. They're kept in safe places, looked after. They never go wanting. They certainly don't have to resort to manual labor to take care of themselves."

Koa tried to imagine what that would be like, to have people keeping him safe and comfortable, bringing him everything that he wanted. It sounded nice. But then he'd never have learned how to swing on a rope or tie a knot. He'd never have tested his weight on a ladder he bound himself, and have known that it would hold anyone who traveled on it. He'd never have swung out over the water, fishing with Tug. "I like my job," he said, half to himself.

"And you're very good at it." Maiel reached over and brushed the back of one wing along Koa's. His breaths sounded suddenly tense and hungry. "I could tell as soon as I saw you. Such strong limbs and broad shoulders. But it isn't right that you and your family should be kept out of the other kingdoms. When I think about what your life must have been like, slaving away every day just for enough food to keep fed, going home to a tiny hovel filled with—how many brothers and sisters have you got?"

"Twelve. But it's not a hovel, it's a—" He remembered the grand houses in the Crown, and the home that Maiel had grown up in, and faltered. Maybe he *had* grown up in a hovel. He knew his family was poor, but they'd never *felt* poor.

"Twelve!" Maiel breathed in fascination. "A house with fourteen other people living in it, scrapping for room, never knowing a moment's peace. I can't even imagine it."

"It isn't so bad." This line of conversation was beginning to make Koa distinctly uncomfortable.

"But of course not. It's all you've known. You can't imagine what it would be like to live in the Upper Kingdoms, to have all the benefits and blessings that we do. But you *should*. Your family should have access to all that I have. It's only fair." Maiel was speaking faster now, staring past Koa as if talking to himself, his brow furrowed in a look of determination. "Only flying foxes can pass through the barrier, of course, but perhaps my father can grant your parents and siblings some kind of token. I know we can find a home for you and your family up here. I have spare funds enough tucked away for something decent, I expect. We could move them up here in a month or two, and then people would see, they'd understand that the lower classes are not just—"

"Wait a minute, wait a minute!" Koa interrupted him. "What do you mean, move my family up here? They're otters! They won't want to come up into the Upper Kingdoms."

Maiel gave him a puzzled frown. "Just because they're otters? Surely you don't believe all that propaganda about how everyone should know their place."

"No—what? No, but don't you see? They *have* their place. They're happy there. *We're* happy there."

"You think you're happy," Maiel said slowly. "But that's only because you don't know everything that you're missing. You don't know what a life without need can be like. If your family were up here, you'd see. Parties every week. Food and drink like you haven't imagined. A life made easy by magic. There are a thousand things you never knew you needed. What about doctors who can spell sickness away? What about education? What about the chance to travel and see the world? If you and your family would just move up here for a while, just try it, you'd realize how miserable your lives really are."

"We're not miserable!" Koa shouted, his blood hot in his cheeks. Maiel flinched at the tone of his voice, but Koa didn't care. "My family is happy, and if you sat down for dinner with them one night, or if you saw how they care for each other and help each other and even fight with each other, you'd know it. They're fine without all the magic and wealth that you think is so mudding great. Maybe to the outside they look strange and broken, but they work. They don't need fixing!"

Maiel hunched down behind his wings, looking hurt. "That's not how I meant it," he said defensively.

Koa swung slack, letting his illusory wings hang loose. He felt suddenly very tired. "I think maybe I should go home. I don't belong up here."

"You could," Maiel said. "If you wanted to."

"I was acting like a such a big shot. You shouldn't have let me go on pretending all that time. I must have been so embarrassing."

"No. You were… you were sweet. And kind of cute. And besides, you were having such a good time."

"And you let me just jump off the branch like that!"

"I didn't exactly expect you to risk your life, you know. Why on earth did you just drop off into nothing? Even experienced foxes look before they launch."

Koa grimaced. "The spell was wearing off. It only lasted four hours, and I didn't want you to see that I'd—" He frowned. How long had he been up here, now? It didn't feel like four hours, but then neither had last night. "What time is it right now?"

"I'm afraid I've no idea," Maiel said. "My pocket watch was in the coat room last night when the accident happened."

The fur lifted on the edges of Koa's wings. "Accident? What accident?"

"But you must have heard! Someone got seawater into the coat room last night. I suppose it was after you left."

"Seawater?" Koa frowned. "But how could anyone do that?"

Maiel shook his head. "I don't know, but Father thinks it must have been some sort of conjuration. He said it looked like the whole room had been submerged. All the enchantments in it were destroyed, of course, even the ones that had grown the room together. There's just a big hole there now—you must have seen it when you came up." He leaned toward Koa with a look of concern. "Look, are you all right?"

Koa barely heard the question. His skin crawled with fright. "Maiel, you've got to get back to your house, quick!"

"Go back? Whatever for? You're behaving strangely, Koa, even for you."

"The parcel! The parcel I left for your father. I'm afraid it might have some kind of enchantment inside."

"Enchantment? But in our house, that could—" Maiel stared at him, his eyes going suddenly wide and frightened. "Koa, what have you done?"

"I didn't know, I swear!"

Maiel bit back a few frustrated phrases and then spread his wings and dropped from the branch, fluttering away.

Koa turned and hurried back toward the Crown, but even with the magic granting grace to his steps, it was difficult to hurry while hanging upside down from branches. With each move forward, he swayed backward and forward, and had to time his steps with the swinging of his own body. By the time he made it to the top of the Crown, he could not see Maiel, though of course at night it was more difficult to spot things at a distance. However, from a distance came shouting and indistinct cries for people to brighten the lights.

Frightened, not certain what to expect, he scrambled across the woven paths as quickly as he was able, and before he had even reached the Kites, glowlamps were rising all around, a crowd of curious bats gathering in the direction of the great, curving lilac walls of Toller's house. A small figure, surely Maiel, fluttered toward a window in the side. The walls blushed with the soft light of the glowlamps within. There was silence.

Koa held his breath for a moment, then let it out, feeling silly. Surely the parcel was nothing sinister. He'd have caused a big row and a scare for nothing.

But then, at the base of the home, one of the inner lights winked into darkness, and then another higher up. Then another. A low rumble shook the Beards, and it seemed to Koa that the entire Crown bent forward, as though caught in a stiff breeze.

A fluttering bat shape burst from one of the nearer windows. "Fly!" Maiel's voice cried, clear and shrill in the night. "Fly away, quickly!"

The other flying foxes muttered amongst themselves. Koa hurried toward them—even if he wanted to escape, he couldn't fly, and the only path that he knew led downward was past the crowd.

Water burst from one of the lower windows in a long jet that arced outward, raining down on the branches below. Screams went up from the crowd, and then another fountain blasted from another window, and another.

The frightened flying foxes scattered, bumping into each other and shrieking as they took to the skies in a mass of brown fluttering, like dead leaves scattering out toward the heavens. Koa could only watch in paralyzed horror as the whole home shook and swayed, filling with what must have been seawater. The petal walls of the home separated, pouring out a great flood. Water vomited out into the Crown, and any place it gushed or spattered, it dissolved the enchantments that wound and bound the branches of the Crown together. Whipping and lashing, the limbs of the great tree untied themselves, frayed holes opening up in the canopy. Larger branches groaned, creaking as they tugged against the spells that had bound them for centuries.

Koa's spot was far enough away that none of the water could reach him, but he hurried all the same, scrambling down the path, around the Kites and toward the passage that led down to the Head. The branches beneath him bucked and swayed, tossing him from his feet several times, and he had to lie flat and cling until they stilled. From below, he could hear screams and shouts as the raining water filtered down to the lower levels.

He scanned the skies for Maiel, hoping he'd managed to escape, but the air was filled with the zigzagging flights of scores of bats.

With a moan, one massive Arm of the Beards—curved by the work of magicians over centuries into a pleasing and artful arc— straightened, hurling itself toward the sky and flinging the dark shapes resting in its fingers into the night.

Koa shuddered in horror and dismay. He had done this. He had done all this. He wasn't sure whether shame or the restless swaying of the Beards made his stomach turn. He dared one last look at Maiel's house and saw it lean heavily toward one side, water gushing out of every window and streaming through the widening separations between its walls. The entire home drooped like a wilting flower, sagged, and finally collapsed, dropping out of sight over the edge of the Beards. Splashing and more screams came from below, followed by crunching, splintering sounds. What had that been? Maiel's bed, perhaps? His father's desk? Koa hoped no one had been injured when it fell.

He didn't want to be standing around here when Maiel came back. How could he explain what he'd done? How could he look Maiel in the eyes after effectively destroying his home and all his possessions? He couldn't. So he slunk along the path, following it down into the Head.

Below, everything was chaos. Foxes hurried away from the great holes that the streaming seawater had opened up in the enchanted floors. For the most part, none of them flew, instead stepping and crawling carefully to avoid the enchantment and flight-nullifying seawater that still rained from above. A few were drenched, their fine clothes—fastening magics undone—matting to their limbs or hanging off of them. They fussed about, rubbing at jewelry or shaking stopped watches at their ears.

Along the broad expanse of one Arm lay the crumpled ruins of Maiel's home, massive lilac petals drooping over the edge, torn and ruined, covering lumps of furniture. A sodden pile of books lay smashed under the edge of one petal. Large, curved shards of colored crystal lay strewn along the Arm. In the middle of the mass, the great metal gears and hoops that Koa had seen whirling in the main room lay in a broken heap, one narrow cog embedded deep into the travel-worn bark of the Arm.

Numb and lost, he turned from it, trying to shut out the cries of the foxes, the groaning of the tree as it shifted under its altered weight. He just wanted to get away from everything, from this whole night. But he had nowhere to go. If anyone from the Upper Kingdom recognized him, or found out what he'd done—or if Maiel told anyone—there would probably be criminal charges. He'd be arrested.

He hurried down the path, keeping his eyes lowered, not daring to let any passersby see his face. Arrested. The thought shook him. He'd almost certainly be imprisoned, or maybe even worse. No one was executed in the Kingdoms anymore, but they could still put you away for the rest of your life. Or exile you.

People bustled past him, and he tried to look unsuspicious somehow, but he wasn't sure what unsuspicious looked like in a situation like this. Hopefully everyone would be too anxious to pay him any attention. Many were taking to the air now, flapping off out of the confines of the branches. He wished desperately that he could follow them. Instead he hurried on foot.

Finally, he reached the winding path that would lead down to the Nets and the footpaths below. He stared down into the darkness below and realized he wasn't sure where he would even go.

Home? He'd bring shame on his whole family. He had let them all down, Tug most of all. Hadn't Tug practically begged him not to deliver that parcel? And instead Koa had left him for some stupid dream that he'd had no right to. And worst of all, he'd stolen Tug's dream when he left. He could never face any of them again.

No. He'd have to leave. He'd take one of the family's boats—another wrongdoing to regret, but not one half so terrible as everything he'd already done—and row someplace. North, perhaps. He could disappear into the mountains of Terai. It would be cold, and lonely, but did he deserve any better?

Still, he couldn't think about leaving right now. Everything that had happened was too new, too sudden. He could scarcely believe any of it; it was like a dream that he still hoped to awake from. He slumped down against the side of the path, hugging his knees with his wings. Maybe it hadn't really been his fault. Maybe it hadn't had anything to do with the parcel he'd delivered. He couldn't have known what would happen. Maybe people would understand.

But no, of course they wouldn't. He wished he knew why Ruduuk had asked him to do this. In vengeance, maybe? Or maybe the lizard had been telling the truth the whole time, and this was some attack from those enemies he'd ranted about.

"I'm in a current too swift for my tail," he groaned.

"An odd expression," said a deep voice near him.

Koa turned his face upward and saw a tall, elegant-looking bat, dressed in fine purple clothes and silver jewelry. He had alluring, exotically handsome features. His eyes flashed with recognition. "You!" the bat hissed.

Koa gaped as old, forgotten remembrances pushed at him, carrying the smells and strains of events that had almost slipped utterly from his memory. "You!" The flying fox was instantly familiar, though Koa's memory of him was dulled and faded by the passage of many years. This was one of the partygoers he'd remembered from the balls he'd attended long ago, back before Atlas had fallen into the Drowned Kingdom. Koa remembered being so fascinated with him, following him about the party, entranced by the way his silver never fell nor twisted, even though they'd been hanging from the branches. But that would have been fifteen years ago at least, and this fox looked young, close to Koa's own age. "How do you know me?" Koa asked wonderingly. He felt suddenly charged with electricity, a heartbeat away from his own broken past.

The exotic bat bared his needle fangs. "I've mistaken you for someone else," he said, and turned to leave.

"Wait!" Koa stood and reached for him, catching him by one wing and spinning him around. "I'm sure I remember you. I—" He sniffed. There was a strange scent on the other bat, far more recently familiar than the bat himself. It was sweet, unpleasantly so, with a chemical edge that sent Koa's stomach turning. "You're enchanted!"

The bat's bronze eyes narrowed. "I should have known you'd see through it. You're like me—too clever for your own good."

"Ruduuk?" Koa's mind whirled. Nothing was making sense anymore. "But how did you get up here? The barrier—"

"Is gone, thanks to your little delivery. I knew that old fool Toller kept the source of the spell in his home. I just needed someone to get to it for me."

"But why? What do you want?"

"That's none of your concern."

Koa could dimly see Ruduuk hiding behind the enchantment now, his haughty expressions twisting the furred muzzle, bronze eyes narrowing in the same way as Ruduuk's own red, reptilian eyes. "But it *is* my concern!" he shouted. "You did this to me. You made me—made me—" He glanced around to make sure no one was listening and continued in lowered tones. "You made me wreck Maiel's home. Everything's in chaos. Part of the Crown is completely gone!"

"That won't matter," sneered Ruduuk, and then drew himself up, stretching his conjured wings. "Oh. Oh, I see. You're worried about your life after this, aren't you? Yes, of course you are. You're a sensible bat, after all, even if you sometimes make foolish bargains. So what are you going to do? Run off and tell someone? That wouldn't be very wise."

"Why not?"

"Why not? Well, whatever could you hope to gain from it, dear boy? After all, it was you, wasn't it, who brought rogue magic into the home of a high magician? No excuse will get you around that. You'll be imprisoned. Hunted. Whereas I have my magic. I'll disappear behind breezes and beneath shadows and be gone."

"Not if I come back with seawater."

Ruduuk gave him a thin smile. "You've done quite enough of that already, haven't you? But no. I have a better plan for you. An offer. And all it will cost you is your silence. Go away and speak nothing of this."

"What could you possibly offer me that would be worth that?" Koa demanded.

"Only this." Ruduuk bowed low, reaching into his purple cloak. When he stood upright again, he held in one wing the cut-glass bottle from his shop. Its milky contents shifted and shimmered in opalescent colors.

Koa stared at it longingly for a moment, then shook his head. "You think you can buy me off with that? A few lousy spritzes of enchantment?"

Ruduuk chuckled and shook the bottle with a flourish, making the liquids within swirl and glimmer more brightly. "Oh, but you see, boy, there are *two* ways to use this potion. The first, on your skin, as you have done twice before: a passing glamour, an illusion that flickers and fades. But sip from the bottle, and the potion *changes* you, muscle and bone. Not for a few hours, not for a night, but forever."

Koa froze. "Forever?"

"Think of it. You could take a new shape, one that none here knows. You could live with your kind, with your *people*, for the rest of your life. You would be handsome, elegant, loved by them. *Whole*. No more scars. No more disgusted looks. And with a little practice, you could even learn to fly. Everything you've ever wanted is in one taste of this bottle. And all you have to do is walk away." The great lizard huddling within the guise of a bat grinned at him, wider than bats could grin. His eyes glittered with a red tinge.

Koa reached for the bottle, his fingers trembling. What would be so different in taking the offer? He'd been about to walk away a moment before, hadn't he? He'd been ready to leave for distant lands, to put his life and his family behind him. Why not simply stay and have everything? Maybe, given time, he could even rejoin his family, one by one, and explain things. He could find a way to make them understand.

But no. Something was wrong with the idea, something sick and unpleasant. He'd be walking away from more than just his life, even more than his family, but he didn't know quite what that was. Something deeper, something more important. He took another look at the bottle, and now he saw an unpleasant luster to the contents. The shifting liquid looked greasy, almost poisonous. Suddenly he wanted nothing to do with it.

"No." He dropped his wing to his side.

Ruduuk wrinkled his illusory muzzle in fury. "So be it. But know for the rest of your pathetic, miserable life that you missed your one chance—that you could have fixed yourself."

"I don't need fixing." Koa declared. "I'm not broken."

He held his breath in wonder at the words that had fallen from his mouth.

Ruduuk, however, snarled, and lunged for him. "Oh, but you will be."

Koa stumbled backward, startled, but he was too slow. Claws too sturdy and powerful to be at the top of a bat's wing closed around his neck. He kicked his feet as Ruduuk hefted him into the air with one wing. The bat-lizard's powerful grip choked him, and he clutched at his neck, struggling to breathe.

"You've still got a pretty little set of wings," Ruduuk said. With long strides, he moved to the edge of the Arm, dangling Koa over the darkness below. "Let's see if you can fly." And with a powerful swing of his wing, he flung Koa into the abyss.

For the second time in as many nights, Koa plummeted toward the Nets. He spun head over heels, his stomach dropping. He knew he couldn't count on landing in a net; they were sparser this close to the trunk. But he had two things this time that he hadn't the night before: lights to orient himself, and whole wings. He stretched them out wide and felt them catch the air, orienting him right-side up. He was still dropping fast, but at least he could see which way he was falling. In panic, he pushed his wings together like an otter clapping his paws. No, that was wrong, but it still gave him a little lift. *Your body is built for flying, It knows how, if you let it take over.*

Below, a gnarl in the trunk of the Beards rose swiftly toward him; he would be dashed against it within a second or two. He didn't have time to focus or concentrate. The moments it would take him to reach for instinct would kill him. Fear flooded his limbs, made his heart race. He flapped his wings as hard as he could and tried not to die. He rose and pushed forward. Rose and pushed forward. At least it *felt* like he rose—he was still falling, but at least he was slowing his descent. Below and before him, the vast brown landscape of the Nets stretched, its tented hills and weighted valleys just out of reach. He would fall right past them to his death. In desperation, he fluttered toward them as quickly as he could. Up and forward. Up and forward. Safe purchase hovered before him, tantalizingly out of reach. But no, that was him. *He* was hovering. His descent had nearly ceased. The air filled the membranes between his fingers and tugged at them, stretched them.

A thrill of elation shot through him—he was flying, actually flying! But all his efforts to reach the Nets would not be enough. Though he was moving forward, it was only slowly, a foot or two with each flap of his wings, and already he was exhausted. The muscles in his chest ached in protest; they were unaccustomed to this sort of movement. He sank lower and lower, watching safe purchase rise just out of reach. If he could just grasp onto one strand, one cord, he would be safe.

With his remaining strength, he pushed his wings down and back, catching the air between his fingers and hurling it behind him as hard as he could. He shot forward and dropped at the same time, his head pitching toward the ground. He clenched his toes in fright… and felt coarse rope between them. A half-second later he swung forward with a jolt, dangling by one foot from the very edge of the Nets. The dark world of the Beards pitched back and forth below him.

Carefully he swung himself up and caught the rope with his other foot, and then pulled himself upright. He panted atop the coarse lines of rope, but didn't dare stop. He pushed himself forward, crawling along the bouncing surface to the footpath. There, he huddled against the bark, willing his heart to stop pounding.

By the time he finally managed to relax, the wind had begun to rise, making the branches around him sway and the leaves rustle. The air in his lungs and on his body felt heavy and thick, like that of an approaching storm.

He stood and felt a warm gust tug through his fur and catch at his wings, nearly pitching him from his feet. Down the footpaths of the Beards was home, and he wanted nothing more than to hurry there to settle in his room and pull his bedsheet over his head and pretend that nothing had happened. But Ruduuk was up in the Head, or even the Crown, now, and who knew what he might do there, what further terrible plans he might have invented.

It was Koa who had delivered the his enchanted parcel. It was Koa who had brought devastation to the Beards. He couldn't leave now, at least not without warning everyone. Drawing his wings close, he gripped the rope ladder that led back up toward the Head and began to climb.

The wind grew steadily stronger, and the sky darker. No moon was visible in the gloom, nor any stars, and in the darkening night even his night vision proved of little use. The only illumination came from distant glowlamps that faintly outlined the shape of the trunk and the rungs above him. Soon, Koa found he had to grope for each step. He hadn't climbed far at all before a sudden burst of wind caught in his wings and nearly tore him from the ropes. In panic he hunched down, folding his wings as tightly to his sides as he was able, and waited for the wind to die down. But it seemed only to grow stronger and gust more often.

This was a definitely a storm, and it had come seemingly out of nowhere. Storms in the Kingdoms could rise swiftly and suddenly, but the rainy season was not due for months. Something terrible was happening.

Koa reached up to climb another step, and again the wind caught in his wing, swaying him sideways and slamming him against the bark of the Beards. He gritted his teeth and climbed higher. But with every step, the storm winds grew stronger and more perilous. He could make it, he thought, if not for his wings. But one more sturdy gust could tear him away from the ladder and fling him out into the open air, and there he would have no chance of flying to safety again. There was only one thing left he could do. He climbed down.

Down the rope ladder, past the Nets, he put his feet on solid bark once more and huddled low. The Bearded Kingdom creaked and swayed in the winds. Keeping close to the bark and crawling on all fours, he made his way down the footpaths into the Lower Kingdom.

The paths were abandoned, which was normal for this time of night, but even considering the hour, they were emptier than usual. Doors of homes and shops had been shut tight, and some people had apparently risen from their sleep long enough to shutter up their windows. Shop signs and hanging glowlamps swayed and clattered in the wind. Papers and clutter blew and whirled along the paths in odd trains, like lost flocks of migrating birds.

He folded his ears back and kept going. The farther he descended, the less fiercely the wind howled; it was definitely highest up near the Head. He tried not to think about what that might mean.

Chapter 12

Down at the Toes, the water was choppy and dark. The boats moored there swayed and creaked at the ends of their lines, straining for freedom in the storm, crashing into each other and the docks as they careened back and forth. Koa headed down the rocking planks of one dock, and the wind hit like a hammer, knocking up a spray of seawater. The drops burned wherever they touched Koa's skin, like hot pepper on the tongue, and he looked down to see tiny holes appearing in his wings and spreading patches where his fine clothes were dissolving, leaving coarse canvas behind. The seawater was melting away his enchantment.

He stood on the edge of the dock, staring out into the open sea. His toes gripping the planks tightly, he spread his wings one last time, feeling the whole flesh tug between his fingers, the delightful stretch as the wind caught at it and tried to lift him. He focused on every sensation—the smoothness of the membranes, the pull in his chest muscles, the way he felt impossibly light and yet helpless, at the whim of the world's breath. Each of these sensations he stored in his memory so that he would never forget them.

Then he dropped to his knees and plunged his wings into the seawater lapping up over the dock. It stung, as though the wounds were fresh and agonizing at the touch of salt. He flattened himself to the planks, soaking his chest with the water, and pushed his arms deeper, gritting his teeth at the pain. A wave rolled at the dock and struck him in the face, forcing the sour smell of salt water up his nose, his ears growing heavy with soaking fur.

When he stood again, his wings were a familiar mass of scars and torn flesh once more. Dark ribbons of useless membrane dangled from twisted bone. He spread his limbs wide, and wind gusted through the rents in his wings. It barely tugged at them at all.

He turned and saw an otter standing just behind him, worrying his paws.

"Breezy? What are you doin' out here? You might not have observed it what with the little splash you were havin' just now, but there's an awful great storm whippin' up, and it's gonna be a choppy boat ride back home."

"Tug." Under any other circumstances, Koa would have been glad to see him. "Look, I'm sorry, but I can't go home right now."

The otter creased his brow in naked dismay. "You mean you've got to go back up there."

"Yes, but—"

"Even if they all treat you bad. Even if it kills you."

"Tug, you're not listening."

"No, *you* listen!" The otter shouted, balling his fists at his sides. Rain streamed back from his face in the wind. "I dunno what they got up there that's so great. I prolly ain't gonna get to see it ever. And I know you think you belong up there because, you know, you're a bat and all. But in all your life, I never seen you ashamed of what you are. And if they make you feel like that, then they're poison, Breezy. They ain't friends, and they sure as mud ain't family. You can buy up all the enchantments you want, but you can't cover up who you are, and that may be part bat, but it's also part otter, and Mum and Dad are worried to death and Ally and Demel and Syrus and Lissie and Eliva are all out lookin' for you, and Oko and Balan and Teel are cryin' and Mak and Ruko and Yuko are takin' care of 'em and tellin' 'em everything's gonna be okay, but everyone's really worried, and they're all a part of you, Koa, and you can't just let 'em go or forget about 'em. You just can't. You can't just buy a spell and make us all disappear. You—you know?" He let his paws drop and gave Koa a helpless stare.

Koa shook his head. "I know. I'm so sorry, Tug. I wish so much I'd never taken that pearl. You've no idea."

"You think this is about the pearl? I woulda just given it to you if you'd come to me. Well. Actually, we probably woulda had a scrap, and there woulda been some nasty words, and maybe a few days of bein' mad, but eventually, I woulda given it to you! This ain't about that. It's about you, and how I'm scared you're gonna go away forever."

"Tug, I'm not—" Koa looked up toward the top of the Bearded Kingdom. The whole tree appeared to be whipping in the wind like a sapling. Dark bits of debris tumbled down from the canopy. *I'm not going to go away forever* had been what he was going to say. But he couldn't promise that. Not now. "I know," he said instead. "I am who I am. I'm Koa of the Drowned Kingdom and I'm Koa of the Toes of Titan. And I don't need a spell to hide that."

Hope lit Tug's eyes, and Koa hated himself for having to squash it. "But—"

Tug sagged. "But you're still going back up there."

"Yes."

"But why?" He spread his webbed paws wide as if to hold back the senselessness of it all.

Koa sighed. "You were right about Ruduuk. He's done something terrible with that parcel I delivered, and I think he means to do worse. He's up there now—"

"I knew it! I knew he was a no good mucksucker! But he can't be up there now, what with the barrier."

"There's not a barrier. Not anymore. Thanks to me. So now I've got to go up and try to stop him, or at least warn people."

Lightning forked across the sky, followed by a terrific crack of thunder. Tug looked up. "I think they may have had several small clues already. But you can't go up there. You'll get whooshed off to open sea!"

Koa shook his tattered wings grimly. "Not without wings, I won't. Anyway, I have to go. I caused this mess."

"No you ain't. Ruduuk did it, you said."

"Tug, there's something else. Ruduuk—he was disguised as a bat."

"Yeah? Like you were then, I reckon. So what?"

"So I've seen that bat before. When I was a little kid. Back when—back before the Great Storm. And all the bats up there say that it wasn't a natural storm. That someone, you know, called it up."

Tug froze halfway through a dismissive nod, his eyes widening. He had to shout over the roaring winds. "Wait. Are you sayin' that you think that *he* did it somehow? Just conjured up a big wind and ripped Atlas out by the Toes?"

Koa stared up into the storm. Great spiral clouds swirled around the top of the Bearded Kingdom, flickering and blooming with hidden lightning. "I think so. I think he killed my family."

"But that means—" Tug followed Koa's gaze. "Hang on, you really think he means to bring down the Beards? But why? Ain't he up there, too? He'd have to be insane."

"Yeah, maybe. But that's why I have to go back up. I have to try to stop him." Koa gave Tug a sad smile and stepped past him.

Tug grabbed his shoulder. "Koa, no. Why's it gotta be you? What can you do? You're just… I mean, you're *you*, and they've got wizards and magic and such. What can you do that they can't?"

Koa hefted a coil of sturdy rope from the dock, tucking it under one wing. "I can tie a mean knot," he said. "And besides—they've all got wings. Maybe I'm the only one who can do anything."

"You said the barrier's gone? Like, anyone can just traipse in or out right now?"

Koa nodded.

Tug gave his shoulder a firm squeeze. "Then you ain't goin' alone."

"I—" Koa stumbled over a dozen weak protests. *This is my mess. I betrayed you. You'd only get yourself hurt.* But he was afraid, and the thought of having Tug along was deeply reassuring.

"I'm coming," Tug said. "You don't get a say."

Koa sagged in relief. "Thank you."

Chapter 13

By the time they reached the top of the footpaths, the wind was so loud they couldn't speak to each other. Doors and shutters clattered, and the whole tree swayed back and forth alarmingly, making Koa's stomach pitch every time it changed direction. Now and then a smaller limb tore away from one of the arms and went crashing toward the sea below.

Despite his earlier bravado, Tug looked terrified, and clung to every step as though he might be plucked away by the wind and hurled off into the night. Koa had tied the two of them together with a bit of rope, assuring Tug that his powerful claws could keep them both from being carried away, though privately, he wasn't entirely sure he could. He found the climb up much easier than his previous descent, however: the tears in his wings prevented the wind from catching at him too forcefully. He still tried to keep his limbs as close to his sides as he could, especially when climbing the rope ladders, which thrashed in the storm like a fishing line with a catch on the end.

They climbed past the point where the dispelled barrier would have resisted Tug, and higher and higher still, until finally Koa reached the branch that would take him into the great, green caverns of the Head. He swung out onto the hanging pathway, clinging with his toes. The wind made each step forward a strain, but he could manage, he thought.

There was a pull at the rope tied around his chest. He looked back and saw Tug clinging to the top of the ladder, staring along the path with a look of terror.

"What's wrong?" Koa called back to him.

"You mad?" Tug shouted. "I can't swing along that like some kinda monkey. I got webbed paws! I'll fall!" He waggled his stubby fingers at Koa.

Koa grimaced. Tug was right. He would have difficulty grasping the branches in the middle of a calm, dry day, and now the wind was high and the branches slippery with rain. Not to mention how exhausted the otter would be after swinging from his paws for several hundred feet. "It's the only way up. You'll have to wait here."

"No way. I ain't leavin' you."

"Well, what do you want me to do?"

Tug shrugged, making the rope between them bounce. Koa stared at it. He fought down a feeling of dread at what he was about to suggest. "Do you trust me?" he called to Tug.

"Course I do." The otter put a lot of bravado into the words, but fear glittered in his brown eyes.

Koa kept his toes tight in their grip on the branches. "Then it's time to go fishing."

Tug's ears went back. "You ain't honestly plannin' to have me bobbing below you like a lure!"

"I can hold you. And the rope's sound, don't worry. Just make sure it's good and snug around your waist and legs and hold on tight."

"Twelve save me." Tug gave a trembling stare down into the darkness below him, climbed down as low as he could go, and released the ladder, gripping onto the rope with both paws.

The cord bit into Koa's chest and limbs, jolting him so hard it forced the breath out of him. He sucked in air through clenched teeth, tugging and pulling at the makeshift harness that ground into his skin, but he could barely budge it. At least it seemed secure. He looked down for Tug and saw the otter clinging to the end of the rope, curled up in a small, terrified ball.

"By the Twelve, you're mudding heavy!" Koa shouted down. "What've you been eating, whole tuna?"

Tug stared up at him, the whites showing all the way around his wide brown eyes. If he said anything, his words were stolen by the storm. The wind swung him about at the end of the rope.

Neither of them would be able to manage this for long. Koa needed to find safe ground. He waited for Tug's weight to swing forward and used the momentum to take his first step. He curled his toes around the next branch and gripped. The wet bark chafed at his skin. Tug swung back and then forward again, and Koa took his next step, and the next. Already he was exhausted. But there was still a long way to go.

He squinted into the rain and wind, trying to take his mind away from his pain and his exhaustion, finding the rhythm. Swing, pause, step, swing, pause. Swing, pause, step, swing, pause. It would have been faster to leave Tug behind, he realized. Without having to carry his brother, he might be already have found Ruduuk and stopped whatever the hedge lizard was up to. But as painful and wearying as Tug's weight was, Koa found having him along reassuring, an anchor in the storm.

Again he looked down at the otter who clung to the rope, eyes squeezed closed, legs twitching in the rude harness. The cords must have been painful to Tug, considering how they sawed into Koa's chest and wing limbs with every swing. *If I'd had wings, I could never have carried him. They'd get in the way, and I wouldn't be able to tie the rope around myself.* The pain seemed to lessen.

The rope itself was stiff with salt. Koa was sure it would hold, though it had plainly been knotted, untied, and knotted again dozens of times. Every knot weakened a rope. But if you never tied a rope to anything, it was useless. Strong, perhaps. Durable. But meaningless. This was well-woven, tightly braided, made of sturdy fibers of manila hemp. It would hold.

Tug yelped from below, and the line jarred as he swung into something. They had reached the edge of the hanging path, and it had led them to a gently sloping branch that descended to the floor of the Head.

In relief, Koa sidled up to the path and let go of the branches with his toes. Tug slid down the slope, tumbling, the line winding around him as he rolled. He yanked Koa after him, and the two of them skidded and bounced into a tangled pile at the edge of the branch.

Tug emitted a low, whimpering moan. "You coulda warned me."

"Sorry." Koa pushed himself upright, untangling himself from loose loops of rope. He tried to undo the knots around his chest, but they were too tight, and the rope had shrunk in the rain. "You got your knife?" He looked around for Tug.

The otter was upside down on his back, his feet and tail dangling over his head. "Ugh. Think so." He patted around his shorts, fished out his oyster knife and passed it to Koa.

It wasn't razor-sharp, but it was sharp enough. Koa wedged it between the knots and sawed them open. Then he cut Tug free.

"Ooogh. 'Bout cinched me legs off, that did. Toes are all gone prickly."

Stabbing pain wracked Koa's own toes. He looked down and flinched—they were slick with blood and torn flesh. *Now they match my wings*, he thought darkly. He nudged Tug. "Come on. We can't spare any time. I'll make sure that wherever we go next doesn't require any more hanging."

"You know me, Breezy. Never one to complain. But I'll take it."

Koa scanned the large space of the Head, peering through the wind and rain. At first he thought everyone had evacuated, but after a moment, he made out the dark specks of flying foxes everywhere, huddled flat against the pathways or clinging to branches. The wind was fierce enough that if any of them stood, they were likely to be blown away. But surely the hedge lizard wouldn't be here, just huddling down to avoid the wind. "I don't see Ruduuk anywhere."

"You think he's higher? Up in the Crown, maybe?"

"Maybe." Koa frowned. Where would the hedge lizard go? He had to be the one causing the storm, which meant he'd have to be casting some kind of powerful spell. Maiel would know, surely, but hopefully Maiel had flown away long before the storm began. If anything had happened to him, Koa would never forgive himself. Poor, sweet Maiel, who had trusted Koa, who had let him into his home, who had kissed him so perfectly that night on the—Koa blinked. *All the sorcerers' strongest spells are performed right here, in the heart of magic.* "I know where he is. Come on."

He looped up the rope again and led Tug down the paths, hunching low in the wind, past foxes clinging to the pathways with terrified faces—mothers sheltering their pups beneath their wings; students clutching papers; an elderly bat who gripped with his toes and swung in the breeze unmoving, eyes closed so that he seemed to be sleeping. Koa hoped he wasn't dead.

One finely dressed male looked up as they drew near and reached out to them. The wind caught at his membranes and filled them like sails of a ship. He shrieked in sudden shrill pain, clinging as tightly as he could to the branches, and then a tear opened in one wing. A dark fan of his blood trailed behind him, the tear spread further, and then he let go and the wind snatched him away, leaving behind only a fading scream. Koa shuddered, pressing his own wings tight to his body.

It took a while to find a path higher that Tug could climb, and with every moment, the wind seemed to grow more fierce. By the time they ascended into the Crown, they had to flatten themselves against the bark of the tree, and the roar of the storm was so loud that they could no longer speak to each other even when shouting.

They climbed through the Crown. Some of the fine homes they passed were clearly protected by enchantments that held them solid and stable, but many more had been torn away by the storm, and others were being stripped away branch by branch, room by room. The whole Kingdom rocked back and forth, and the effect was both dizzying and nauseating. What few glimpses Koa could catch of the outside world showed high waves, dark clouds, and lightning bolts. The mosses had been torn away from the Kingdom by the wind; it was Bearded no longer.

Above the Crown, the wind seemed less strong, but there Koa could see no bats. Either they had all flown away earlier or been caught below by the storm. All the fine houses here were still standing, protected from the gale by the magics of the sorcerers who owned them—all but Toller's, of course. A gaping chasm stretched out from the place that that home had once stood, and wild branches jutted and clawed upward in stark contrast to the neatly woven garden that formed the rest of the Crown.

The clouds swirled above, crackling with lightning that flashed deep in their otherwise dark coils. Swirling at the center of this maelstrom was a great hole, like the black socket of an eye staring down at the Kingdom, focused unmoving on the raised hill above the end of the trunk.

There, in the heart of magic, surrounded by the Kites that careened, wheeled, and strained at their tethers, stood Ruduuk, in his lizard form once more. He was stretched taller than Koa had ever seen him stand, his arms raised high over his head, hands twisting and gesturing in broad movements that streaked traces of pale light in the air. His long, purple robes flapped so vigorously in the wind that Koa wondered they weren't torn away from him. The lizard didn't seem to notice them, focused as he was on the magic he conducted through the heart of the tree and into the vortex above.

Koa had no idea what sorts of magic Ruduuk might throw at them as they approached; he could only hope that the lizard was too occupied with his spell to attack them.

"Come on," Tug growled at his side. "We gonna wait for him to tear the Kingdom down? Let's get 'im." The otter streaked forward, a brown blur, keeping his body low to the ground, darting along the paths.

Koa winced. He'd never forgive himself if Tug got hurt. *Lightning*, he thought. *What if Ruduuk can control the lightning as well as the winds?* "Wait!" he called, and raced after.

The wind must have carried his cry to Ruduuk, for the lizard whirled on them, his red eyes glittering as he spotted them. "So, you managed to survive," he roared over the storm. "Reconsidered my offer, then?"

Tug skidded to a halt, looking back with the question in his eyes. Wait? Fight?

Koa waved for him to be still. "You're going to bring down the Beards if you don't stop!" His voice was already hoarse from shouting. "You'll kill everyone! Just like—just like you did with Atlas!"

Ruduuk grinned yellow daggers. "So you sorted that out, did you? Of course you did. You're a clever one. Like me. But last time was an accident. The magic at the heart of Atlas—it drew me in too deep. I wasn't prepared. Couldn't stop the spell. This time will be different. This time I won't fell my Kingdom."

"*Your* Kingdom?" Tug shouted, bristling in the rain. "What makes you think it's yours?"

Ruduuk wheeled his scaled arms in arcane turns as he spoke, the rain matting his robes to them. "Because I'm taking it, you incipient bottom-feeder. The selfish little bats have claimed their enchantments and baubles for far too long. How dare they keep me out of their little paradise? It's unjust. They will have all their other Kingdoms in which to waste away idle hours. This one will be mine." Hunger flashed in his eyes. "So many pretty things. So much gold. So many sparkling jewels."

"You're mad!" Koa cried in disbelief. "You destroyed my home and killed my parents for—for what? For gold? For a room with a view?"

"You think to judge me, boy? Haven't you used my magic to go after the same things? I recall a lovely pearl I don't believe was yours. So where is *your* little otter family now?"

"Right here," Tug declared, and charged Ruduuk, racing up the hill and ducking beneath the ropes that held all the Kites in place.

Lightning cracked the sky, blinding Koa. He stumbled forward, and when his sight cleared, he saw the dark shape of an otter lunging at the lizard on the hill.

Whenever Koa had seen Ruduuk before, it had been in the shop, where the lizard's great height and bulk sent him slouching forward, leaning on the counter, or even crawling on all fours. Here, though, in the open air, Ruduuk stretched to his full stature, his massive tail lending him support. The wind seemed scarcely to affect him at all. So when Tug leapt for him, he turned and snatched the otter out of the air with one powerful swipe of an arm, dashing him to the ground.

Koa was no use in a fight, and though Tug was quick and scrappy, he stood little chance of taking down the massive lizard. They would have to try something else. Koa reached for the little oyster knife he had tucked in his belt. No. It was sharp, but small, and unlikely to penetrate Ruduuk's scales even if he could get close enough to stick it in.

Tug landed on his back and rolled backward, flipping to his feet and springing toward Ruduuk once more. The lizard swiped at him again but missed, stumbling forward, and Tug bent like a greased eel around him, hopping upright and pummeling his side with a series of quick jabs. Ruduuk roared, lashing his tail to one side, but Tug only leapt over it and pounded at his other side.

Koa gaped. He had never seen Tug fight before—his brother was slick and swift, his moves brutally efficient. But it would not be enough, and even if Tug could knock Ruduuk out, they had no assurance that the storm would end. But what could he do? He couldn't fight. He couldn't use magic. He couldn't even fly. All he could do was—he looked up at the sky. The great Kites zigged and zagged in erratic patterns, straining at the ends of their ropes. Even in the storm, they would not crash, as they'd been enchanted to ascend eternally.

His eyes widened. He gripped the rope still tucked under one wing.

The first Kite was near, its cord humming like a strummed lute string as the wind pulled at it. Koa took his rope and looped it around the other. Tying the knot would be difficult—his rope was wet and stiff, and the cord to which he was affixing it jerked back and forth with the movements of its Kite. It was almost an impossible knot. No one else in the Kingdoms could have tied it. It had to be perfect, gripping the other rope tightly without slipping up or down.

And Koa had little time. Tug was fighting valiantly, but his strength would not last. He scrambled up Ruduuk's back, clouting the lizard across the skull with several vicious blows, but Ruduuk reached up and seized him with one arm and slammed him down. Tug got up, clutching his side, dancing from foot to foot, his teeth bared.

One Kite would not be enough; Koa was sure of that. He moved to the next and tied another knot, this one just as tightly as the first, and around the next Kite after that.

Without Ruduuk's gestures to guide the storm, the winds had begun to calm, the great whirl of clouds above the Beards slowing its spin. "What are you going to do when the storm stops, Ruduuk?" Koa called. "The foxes will only come back when they can! You'll have to destroy the whole tree to stop them."

Ruduuk growled, turning, and Tug got in one savage kick at the lizard's knee before Ruduuk shoved him away. "They can try."

But my new barrier will keep them all out. Miserable wretches. They learned that spell from me. Me! They stole it from me and used it against me to keep me from my rightful place."

A fourth Kite tied. Koa hurried around to the fifth.

Tug lunged at Ruduuk again and was struck across the face by one heavy sweep of the lizard's tail. He got to his feet again, staggering, plainly dazed by the blow, and before he could react, Ruduuk fell upon him, pounding him to the ground again with one powerful swing of a fist. Tug groaned, reaching up with one arm, the other dragging against the woven branches of the hill, his feet kicking.

Ruduuk pummeled Tug again.

Tug twitched, one leg kicking.

Koa's fingers slipped on the rope as he struggled to finish the knot.

Ruduuk stood, and Tug did not get up. The lizard raised one taloned foot above the prone otter, his robes whipping in the wind.

Five Kites would have to be enough.

"Ruduuk! You've forgotten something!" Koa called. He ducked under the ropes.

The hedge lizard turned, his red eyes narrowed into slits. "I forget nothing."

Koa stood as tall as he could in the wind, keeping his wings close to his sides. "You've forgotten that I can use magic, too."

"You? Preposterous." Ruduuk sneered, but he turned away from Tug, looking uncertain. Beyond him, Tug gave another groan and rolled onto his side.

Daring a sigh of relief, Koa moved toward Ruduuk. "Is it? I've stepped into the heart of magic. I know what it feels like to have all that power flowing through you. How you never want to leave. I know why you couldn't step out of it before." He reached inside his wing as if to draw something out.

The lizard bounded toward him, in one mighty leap knocking him down. Koa landed on his back, sliding across the wet branches. Like a crocodile, Ruduuk slithered after him, planting one heavy hand on Koa's chest, pressing him into the woven branches. His forked tongue licked the air. With his other hand, he rummaged through Koa's shirt and wings, finding nothing. "And just where is this so-called magic?" he hissed.

Straining to breathe against the weight pressing down on his narrow chest, Koa croaked, straining in vain for the oyster knife that had been knocked from his waistband. It glinted just beyond the reach of his fingers.

Ruduuk glanced contemptuously at the little blade. "That? You think that little thing could hurt me?" He moved forward, shifting his hand to clamp it down on Koa's scarred wing, his hot carrion breath puffing into Koa's face.

Koa squirmed, legs kicking against the flat scales of Ruduuk's belly, toes scratching at the lizard's bare legs. Bat claws were good for gripping, but they were a poor weapon. "No," he gasped. "The magic is in my head. It's in what I know. The future."

Ruduuk snorted. "The future." He shifted again, pinning Koa's wings to the ground with both his hands. "No one can see that."

"I can." Koa strained for breath, struggling with his legs. From one eye, he could see the silhouette of Tug getting shakily to his feet. "You're going to die very soon, far away from here. You'll be alone in the sea. You'll struggle, but your magic will do you no good. You'll drown."

"And what makes you think that?" Ruduuk grinned at Koa, baring rows of pointed teeth.

Tug barreled into his side, knocking him off of Koa. He bellowed in surprise, tail lashing as he rolled onto his back.

Koa pushed himself across the wet branches and snatched up the fallen knife in his wing-fingers. "Because you're like me," he said. He looked down pointedly at Ruduuk's ankle. He'd always been better at tying knots with his toes than with his fingers. He reached up and grasped the finely woven cable, tight as a lute string, that anchored all of the Kites to the hill. He sawed at it with the oyster knife and the fibers of the cable snapped one by one as though desperate to part. "You can't fly."

Ruduuk looked down at his ankle and saw the old mooring rope Koa had tied to it. His gaze followed the rope to each of the five Kites to which it had been firmly knotted. His red eyes went wide. "No," he began, reaching out, and then Koa cut through the last strand of the cable.

It whistled as it whipped through the air, snapped around by the rising Kites that could now pull free of their anchor. The mooring rope trailed upward after them as they rose and yanked at Ruduuk's ankle, wrenching him from his feet. He howled, eyes bulging in terror as he was dragged by his ankle along the ground, past Koa. With taloned fingers he seized the woven limbs of the Crown, clinging in panicked desperation, but the Kites rose higher, stretching him upward until his tail lashed toward the heavens.

"Curse you," he roared into Koa's face. "Curse you and your whole mudding family!"

Koa scrambled backward away from him.

Ruduuk clenched his teeth, howling in pain as the Kites strained to carry him away, his fingers stretching open from their grip.

At last, one hand pulled free. He gave Koa a scowl of unmeasured hatred and let go—

—but his free hand closed around Koa's foot, and the Kites tore them both away from the ground into the stormy skies.

Koa swung dizzily as the Kingdom of the Beards dropped away. Below, Tug, clutching at his side with one paw, reached up toward him. His blood-matted muzzle was parted in shock. He dwindled away into a speck on the massive, thrashing Crown of the great mangrove.

Koa hung from Ruduuk's cool, scaled fingers and the two of them swung out over the Kingdoms, whose great heads, grey in the darkness, now seemed but the size of ordinary treetops. The Kites rose into the storm, buffeted by the winds, and beneath them Koa and Ruduuk were a pendulum, swinging in lurching patterns that made Koa's stomach turn. He tugged and struggled, but Ruduuk's grip on his ankle was steely tight.

Lighting forked past them with a deafening boom, and then they were surrounded by dark grey clouds. The world below disappeared.

"You fool, you miserable fool!" Ruduuk bellowed at him. "You'll die with me. I'll never let you go."

Even if you did, thought Koa desperately, I'd never survive. The water must be thousands of feet below by now. There was no way out. No way home. He wished he'd had a chance to say goodbye to his mother and father, his brothers and sisters. At least Tug would be there to tell them what happened. At least they'd know he went out fighting to save everyone.

He swung free, not fighting anymore, staring into the grey of the night and fog.

Then they were above the storm, the clouds below a swirling, flat mass. Above them, the stars sparkled clear. The air was colder than any Koa had ever felt. The moon looked huge, a radiant white pearl, blindingly bright after the darkness of the storm below.

Something glinted in Ruduuk's robe.

Koa almost paid it no attention, but then it glimmered again, distractingly. He peered up and saw, tucked in the inner pocket of the wet robe that hung against the lizard's side, a little jar of cut glass. *The Eau de Grâce.*

Struggling, he leaned upward, reaching toward the pocket.

Ruduuk bared his teeth. "It's no good fighting," he muttered, his voice heavy and listless. "We're both dead." Then he saw what Koa was reaching for and sucked in breath through his fangs. "No, you don't. That's mine!" He let go of Koa's foot and reached for the pocket.

Koa only just managed to hook the corner of Ruduuk's robe with one finger as he fell. He dropped, pulling the robe down over the lizard's head, and swung out over the clouds. From this far up, they looked like a great, grey grassland.

Ruduuk struggled in the confines of the robe about his head, raking and grasping at Koa. The little glass bottle tipped out of his pocket.

Koa let go of the robe and fell after the bottle. His stomach lurched as he dropped, pitching head over heels. In one quick turn he saw Ruduuk shrinking into a flailing dark speck against the moon, hoisted ever higher by five giant, oddly-shaped kites. In the next, surely by purest luck, he caught the bottle.

He fumbled it in his claws, disoriented by the terrible speed with which he was falling and the loud rush of the wind. The cloud bank rose toward him. Moonlight. He needed moonlight to activate the spell. Once he fell through the clouds, it would be too late.

He pinched the squeeze bulb, but the wind carried the milky liquid away. If any of the tiny droplets touched him, they were not enough. He held the bottle beneath himself and squeezed again, but he rolled in his fall and again the wind took it away. The cloud bank rose beneath him, nearly all he could see.

Desperate, he pinched the top of the bottle in his fingers and unscrewed the little brass cap. A long trail of opalescent fluid rose from the bottle. Towering wisps of grey cloud rose up around him like a ghost of a mangrove forest.

He shoved the end of the bottle in his muzzle and swallowed desperately.

Pins and needles covered his skin. His bones burned with the fire of transformational magic. He felt the tug of wind against his wings and spread them, searching for the memory of how he'd flown perhaps an hour before. He cupped the air between his fingers and pushed downward. Downward. Down. The blinding grey of the clouds surrounded him. If he had slowed his descent at all, he couldn't tell. He flapped as quickly and as hard as he could, but still the air rushed past him. Up and forward. Up and forward.

Then the clouds broke, and open water shifted below. He couldn't see the trees of the Kingdoms anywhere—maybe they were behind him. Maybe the wind had blown him beyond their boundaries. He couldn't worry about that now.

His shoulders ached with exhaustion as he fluttered, the membranes of his wings stretching. The dark sea rose toward him. For a moment, he thought he almost hovered, and then his limbs shuddered with exhaustion, and he pitched and fell.

The ocean struck him like a hammer. Dazed, he struggled beneath the waves, blowing air out through his nose the way Tug had taught him. The water roared in his ears, dark and warm compared to the air he'd fallen from. He kicked his feet hard, cupping his wings around the water and pushing at it the way he had the air, but it streamed between his fingers.

Finally he broke the surface, sucking in a deep, rasping breath. All around was dark. He rode the water, kicking and panting. He wasn't falling anymore, but his situation wasn't much improved. He could swim scarcely better than he could fly. If he couldn't find something to grab onto, he'd drown in a matter of minutes.

He beat at the water with his wings and found that even though he'd drunk the potion, the seawater had broken the enchantment. Twisted flesh hung from his knotted bone fingers. And the bottle was lost for good now, somewhere beneath the ocean, its contents dissolved into the magic-nullifying sea. It was just as well. With whole wings, unwieldy and heavy with water, he wouldn't have been able to swim at all.

Turning in the water, he searched for signs of the Kingdoms, but could see nothing. At least the waves didn't seem to be that high—that suggested that without Ruduuk to maintain it, the conjured storm had faded away. The Beards would be safe.

He was already tiring, exhausted from the climb, the fight, and the flight. Plus he'd had no sleep. His body was wearing out. He sunk lower, struggling to keep his head above the waves. Then, just by him, the dark shape of something glided through the water.

A small fishing boat—or part of anyway, an upended bow, trailing a snapped rope behind it like a water snake. Serves 'em right for using old rope, Koa thought to himself, but he was grateful to whoever owned the boat that they had. He splashed toward it and heaved himself up on the reassuringly solid wood.

The latter half of the boat proved to be gone, splintered boards dragging just below the water.

Reasoning that the direction the boat had come from must be toward the Kingdoms, Koa trailed his feet in the water and paddled, turning the hulk around and pointing it in what he hoped was the direction it had come, though it was too dark to be sure.

With the last bit of his strength, he splashed through the waves.

Chapter 14

It seemed like hours had passed, though Koa couldn't be sure. He could barely summon the energy to move his feet anymore. There was no point anyway. He had not found the Kingdoms. There was the faint glow of the rising sun, so he knew which way was east, but that helped him little, as he could not tell whether he had fallen west or east of the Kingdoms, nor whether he had drifted past them in the night. Besides, a fog had settled over the water, so thick and heavy that he could be right up on his home without knowing it. He had heard that fog only formed near the land, so he might be close, but he had no way of knowing which direction to go, and he was too exhausted to waste energy traveling in the wrong direction. He rested his head on the keel of the boat and felt the rocking of the waves beneath him.

He was lost, completely lost. He wondered how long it would take him to die out here. He stared blindly into the fog all around, uniform and blinding, but for that faint light out to his right.

He lifted his head, his ears perking. A light. It wasn't his imagination. It wasn't the sunrise. It was blurred and glowing in the fog.

With renewed energy, he kicked his feet, steadily shifting the shattered boat toward it. It was definitely a light—pale, cool white, a familiar color. He strained his eyes as the fog cleared.

Blazing through the mist was a glowlamp with a shape carved into it: a flying fox, crudely shaped, its wings spread, smiling. *The way home.*

Koa plunged over the side of the boat and swam toward it with all his remaining strength.

When he finally pulled himself onto the docks, panting and shaking, he saw that both the family's boats were gone. Aside from the glowlamp, the house lights were dark, no candles lit, which meant that everyone was out. He sat, still short of breath, and then lay flat on the planks, staring up at Titan, its great trunk disappearing into the fog. Faintly above, he thought he could see glowlamps, tiny and forlorn in the Upper Kingdoms.

He must have fallen asleep, for he opened his eyes to the knocking of boats against the dock. Wearily, he pushed himself upright, and was summarily buried under a pile of fourteen joyous, cheering otters.

Chapter 15

The sun was hot on Koa's ears as he climbed the pathways of the Crown of the Bearded Kingdom. Even though it was early afternoon, many flying foxes were awake, working on repairing the damage from the storm. Tired-looking magicians moved from house to house, weaving branches back into place, reshaping bark. Carpenters hammered and sawed, building doors and furniture. Food and drink vendors moved carts—some on wheels, some floating—from place to place, offering refreshment to the workers. Not all of the laborers were bats, either: workers from the Lower Kingdoms had offered their services to help restore the Upper. Koa himself had set his skills to repairing ladders and lashes wherever it was needed. The homes, shops, boats and docks below had been damaged as well, and in return, the Head and Crown had sent their magicians to help where they could.

Ten days had passed since the storm had shaken the Kingdoms, and still there was a great deal of work to be done, but the trees would recover. Happily, there had been no loss of life. Many foxes had been injured, or blown out to sea, but beyond the reach of the conjured storm, they'd been able to find a spot to roost until the weather calmed. The only person confirmed missing was Ruduuk, and when anyone spoke of him, it was in uneasy tones.

A few had seen a strange, exotic bat step into the heart of magic and then transform into a hulking monitor lizard. They had seen him move with the magic, and then the wind he'd summoned had forced them all to fly away. No one knew what had happened to Ruduuk after that. Some thought he was still around, hidden somewhere in the gnarls and crannies of the Kingdoms. Others swore that the Twelve had carried him off for his crimes.

Koa didn't know if anyone in the Upper Kingdoms recognized him from the night of the storm. Many stared at him as he passed—but then, that was nothing new. After several days working in the Upper Kingdoms now, he no longer felt uneasy baring his scars around them. Some looked at him with disgust, and most with pity. He didn't mind. Their disgust didn't mean he was ugly, nor did their pity mean he was broken. He was just Koa of the Drowned Kingdom and the Toes of Titan. He let their stares blow through his wings like the wind.

However, he had not yet dared see Maiel. Once or twice while working in the Upper Kingdoms, he had caught a glimpse of him and ducked away. After what he'd done, he didn't know how to face Maiel again.

This morning, a letter had arrived for Koa by messenger. He'd opened it and found only a lavender card with gold calligraphy:

You are cordially invited to attend the Firefly Ball
Saturday Night - Crown of Titan
Come as you are

The paper had smelled like Maiel—sweet lilac, old books, and honey.

176

Koa climbed up above the Crown. The little hill in the center of the tree looked odd without the Kites dancing above it—bald and forlorn. The woven paths had mostly been repaired, but the branches were still stripped free of their leaves and their flowers. Tiny green buds dotted their lengths.

Looking for the great hole in the tree where Maiel's home had been, Koa discovered that it had mostly been closed in: the massive limbs of Titan had been ensorcelled back into place, and even now several magicians stood around the edges, their wings spread as they worked their magic, colorful, fine-spun robes rustling in the breeze. Koa wondered if any of them was Toller.

He made his way down the paths, past the hill where he and Tug had fought Ruduuk, looking about for Maiel. Finally he asked an elderly male if he knew where Maiel could be found, and was directed to the far side of the Crown, where there was a little shaded garden with wicker tables and chairs.

At one of the tables sat a little bat with round glasses and fluffy reddish-blond fur. He was sipping a cup of tea and studying a book with great intensity.

"Lovely garden," Koa said, walking up to the table.

Maiel looked up, blinking. "You should see it when it's in bloom."

Koa looked around at all the stems of flowers, their blossoms torn away. He folded his ears back. "Oh."

"You came. I sort of thought you wouldn't come back."

Koa stared at his toes. "What do you say to a guy after you've knocked his house into the ocean?"

"Oops?"

He looked up.

Maiel gave him an expectant smile. "I mean, unless you intended to."

"You have to believe me. I had no idea that would happen. I—I suppose I should have known something was wrong, but—"

"That wizard who raised the storm told you a few lies, I suppose."

"Yes, and I should have suspected. Tug—my brother—warned me, even, but—"

"But the wizard gave you the enchantment you wanted."

"Yes."

"So you could come and see me."

"Yes."

"In exchange for delivering the parcel."

Koa sighed. "Yes."

Maiel set down his book. "So you did it all for me."

"I—" Koa hesitated. "Mostly. I mean, it *is* a pretty world you live in. I wanted to see it."

"And I told you not to come. It sounds like this is all my fault then, isn't it?"

"What?" Koa looked up in surprise. "Of course not! You didn't know I was going to bring a dangerous spell into the Upper Kingdoms."

"Ah, but *you* knew?"

"I didn't *want* to know. I just wanted to see you again."

"So you risked wild magic and terrible danger just to be with me." Maiel looked up and grinned. "I even hear you make a habit of it. There are stories, you know, of a fox with torn wings and an otter at his side. They say while everyone else was helpless, those two climbed into the heart of the storm, and afterward the storm died away. Whoever would do a thing like that must be incredibly courageous. It's hard to believe that any such person could care what others saw when they looked at him. He'd know deep inside he'd done what no one else could. He'd know he'd saved them all."

Koa's ears burned hot. "Maiel, I—I—I—" He clenched his teeth, took a deep breath and tried to control his stammering tongue. "I never minded so much what anyone else said. But I couldn't bear the thought of this mattering to *you*." And he spread his torn wings wide, exposing their full horror: the white, pink, and black scarring; the twists of flesh; the long hanging ribbons of shredded membrane; the bones that had healed at painful angles; the joints that tore open frequently and seeped.

"But it does matter to me," Maiel said. He let his gaze wander over the desolation of Koa's wings, unflinchingly. Then he stepped forward and put his own wings across Koa's shoulders, squeezing with the fingers that threaded through those perfect sails. "These shoulders, your chest, your arms, so sturdy. From climbing up and down ladders your whole life, I expect. Do you know how strong you are? Do you know how you move? You are like no other bat I've ever seen. It matters to me. It makes you beautiful."

Maiel leaned up and kissed Koa hungrily.

For a moment, Koa thought they must be standing in the heart of magic again, because he nearly lifted from his toes.

He was diving off the edge of a tree branch in the middle of the night.

He was seized up by a Kite and elevated into the clouds.

He was dropping in the moonlight toward the open water thousands of feet below.

He was flying.

About the Author

Ryan Campbell was raised in Arkansas and has six younger siblings and two older parents, none of whom will ever read this if he can help it. He currently lives in the California Bay Area with his husband David. He has previously been published in New Fables, and is working on his second book as you read this, unless it has been published already, in which case, he's probably stopped.

About the Artist

Cooner has been known to draw a line or two. (Over a few decades, all those lines begin to add up.) He is an illustrator, animator, cartoonist, and designer, depending on the needs of the day. More information can be found at http://cooner.johntoons.com.

About the Publisher

FurPlanet Productions is a small press publisher serving the niche market that is furry fiction. We sell furry-themed books and comics published by us and most major publishers in the community. If you can't get to a furry convention where we are selling in the dealers room, visit *www.FurPlanet.com* to shop online.